Tell-Tale Publishing's 5th Annual Horror Anthology

Rob Tucker

Elizabeth Alsobrooks

Darren Simon

Janet Post

Ric Wasley

Francesca Quarto

Robert James

Tell-Tale Publishing's 5th Annual Horror Anthology

Rob Tucker ©The Jungle
Elizabeth Alsobrooks ©Bride of Bazel
Darren Simon ©Resurrection
Janet Post ©The Switch
Ric Wasley ©Rhiannon
Francesca Quarto ©Two for Death
Robert James ©Retribution

Tell-Tale Publishing Group, LLC
Swartz Creek, MI 48737

Printed in the United States of America

Table of Contents

The Jungle

Rob Tucker

"I'm telling you, Preston, there's something wrong with this house."

"What are you talking about? We have a beautiful house, upgrades, new floors, all the latest appliances. We're not wealthy, you know. We can't keep changing things just because you get an itch."

"I'm not talking about the upgrades and appliances. Strange things have started happening."

"Strange things? What kind of strange things?"

"Yesterday, when I opened the utensil draw, a steak knife flipped up out of the knife section and took a swipe at my hand when I was reaching in to get a butter knife."

Preston chuckled. "You think the steak knife was jealous?"

"I'm serious, Preston. This isn't funny. The steak knife deliberately attacked me."

"You probably just pressed the handle and it flipped up."

"No, no, I didn't even touch the steak knives. I'm telling you, Preston, it was like it was waiting for me like a snake and when I reached in, it struck."

"That's absurd, Miriam. We don't live in the jungle where predatory beasts are waiting to attack you. This is a modern home, as if you didn't fully appreciate all the conveniences we have."

"Modern or not, something is happening to this house."

"Don't be ridiculous."

"It's not the first time this has happened."

"What, the steak knife attacking you?"

"That and other things. It started happening when Lionel turned two years old."

"What other things?"

"If I tell you, you'll just belittle me."

"Oh, come on, Miriam. I'm just teasing when I make fun of you. You're a funny person. That's one of the reasons I married you."

"Sometimes I think it's the only reason."

"Of course not. You're a cute obedient woman. Just what I want. You're always polite and you know your place and you do what you're told."

"That's not how we started out."

"Nonsense. You've always depended on what I have to say. You ask my advice all the time. You always listen and agree because I know more about everything than you do. And how come you stopped calling me Press, like I asked? All my friends call me

Press because I can press three hundred pounds at the gym."

"I don't like the sound of it. Your name is Preston."

"But Press suits me better."

"It's admirable that you're so strong but I married Preston, not Press."

"You're being difficult. I don't like it."

"I was thinking I might go back to working at the library on a part-time basis."

"Are you out of your mind? You can't do that. You're a mother. You have to stay home and take care of Lionel and take care of the house."

"We can hire a sitter."

"No, absolutely not. What's gotten into you? I don't want a stranger taking care of my son."

"He's our son."

"That's right and it's your duty to take care of him."

"And cook and do the dishes and the wash and clean the house."

"Yes, and I won't approve anything else. That's why you don't have a personal bank account. I control the finances. And by the way, when's supper? I've had a hard day at the office. I'm starving."

"I haven't had time to fix supper. I've been taking care of Lionel."

"You've always done both since he was born."

"It's different now that he's two."

"You can't use that as an excuse," said Preston.

"It's not an excuse. You try taking care of him yourself all day."

"I don't do diapers. You know that."

"He's potty-trained."

"I don't clean potties."

"It's simple. You just flush the poop down the toilet and rinse out the bowl."

"No thanks. What about dinner?"

"Order something in or go out and eat. I can't make dinner."

"What's the matter? Are you sick?"

"No, the cooking utensils won't let me. They slip out of my hands. And the pots and pans won't do what they're supposed to. The lids keep jumping off and the pots turn over and fall off the stove. Lionel almost got burned on boiling hot water yesterday."

"What? You didn't say anything. Oh, I know why. That's just your clumsiness. You've always been clumsy."

"I have not always been clumsy. These things are happening. I'm under attack constantly. I have to be on my guard all the time."

"All right, show me. Open the utensil drawer. I'll bet you dollars to donuts no steak knife will strike at you like a snake. And I'll bet your pots and pans will nicely cook whatever you put in them."

Miriam walked to the utensil drawer. Prepared to leap back, she slowly and cautiously pulled it open. The steak knives didn't move. None of the forks, butter knives, and spoons moved.

"There, see! Now, pick up one of your cooking utensils."

Miriam did as ordered.

"There, see! All you have to do is grip it firmly. If you hold it loosely, of course, it will slip out of your hand. Now, you don't have any excuse. Get on with dinner. I'm going to have a beer and pretzels and watch the news. Call me when dinner is ready." He grabbed a cold beer out of the refrigerator, popped off the cap, grabbed a bag of pretzels from the pantry cupboard, and stomped into the living room.

The next day, after her husband went to work, the surprise attacks happened again. Only this time, the steak knife didn't come after her because she left the utensil drawer closed with the magnetic baby lock.

In the midst of giving Lionel a bath in the tub, the drain belched a horrendous growl and opened its mouth wide enough to swallow the toddler and suck him down into the drainpipe. With a sharp cry, Miriam grabbed her child and snatched him back as his feet and legs disappeared into the gurgling hole.

Trembling, she toweled Lionel off and put a fresh training diaper on him.

Hoping for a reprieve, she stripped the beds and headed for the laundry room.

Her momentary relief ended when the socket plug shields popped out and hit her like miniature cannon shots as she passed by carrying a load of dirty laundry. Electrical lightning streamed out and shocked her legs. She screamed, dropped the laundry and swept up Lionel following a few feet behind before he could wander into the electrical charges dancing across the room.

She grabbed her car keys off the kitchen counter. Clutching Lionel in her left arm, she headed for the front door as the utensil drawer unlocked itself and the steak knives rose up in mass and flashed after her rattling like a swarm of bees.

"Potty!" Lionel cried. "Potty!"

She smelled the rising poop odor from his diaper. Too late to make it to the potty.

She watched the knives circling above the dining room table organizing in phalanx formation preparing to attack. She tried desperately to open the door but the deadbolt wouldn't budge.

Moaning, she ran down the hall to the master bedroom, and slammed the door behind her. The flying knives thudded into the wooden door.

She dashed to the French doors that opened onto the patio. They did not respond to her jiggling the handle. The house had her trapped. She and Lionel were its prisoners.

She put Lionel on the bed, picked up a small chair and smashed through the glass of the French doors scattering shards everywhere. She grabbed her toddler and, carefully avoiding the jagged edges jutting out of the door frame, stepped through the opening.

The bedroom door flew open. Flipping and whirling in disarray, the steak knives zoomed into the bedroom and out the shattered French doors in pursuit of Miriam, who had dashed around the back of the house to the garage side door.

Inside the garage, she roughly placed Lionel in his car seat, climbed into the driver's seat and pressed the remote. The garage door slowly rose, rattling upward on its metal rollers.

The duration of waiting extended as the door stopped in mid-climb. In the rearview mirror, Miriam saw the suspended door and started the car engine. She would crash through if she had to.

Lionel's screams drew her attention to him in the back. The car seat was slowing wrapping its sides around him.

She leaped out of the car, pulled open the back passenger door, and frantically tried to unbuckle the seat belt. Each time she snapped it open, the fastener snapped back shut. She moved faster than the snap and pulled and tugged her screaming child out through the sides of the constraining web straps. Bending to avoid the low-hanging door, she waddled out of the garage onto the front lawn.

Moments later, sensing where she was, the squadron of steak knives came flying around the corner of the garage and headed straight for her and Lionel. Screeching, she ran behind the thick trunk of an oak tree.

The knives thudded into the trunk, except for one. The one that had first attacked her in the utensil drawer rolled out and circled the tree. It dove and slashed Miriam's free arm, drawing a stream of blood.

Miriam fainted and collapsed at the base of the tree.

When Preston came home from work and pulled into the driveway, he noticed her sitting under the oak tree. She had minor cuts and abrasions on her right arm. Lionel was running around naked on the grass. A full diaper lay next to Miriam.

"What happened?" he asked. "Did you fall down the steps? Were you climbing the tree?"

Miriam glared at him and said nothing.

He asked, "What are we having for dinner?"

Bride of Bazel

Elizabeth Alsobrooks

The air thickened and closed in around them, resisting the forward motion of their car until it seemed the fog's weight rather than loss of visibility slowed their progress.

"Should we pull over, Mehmet?" she asked with a soft tone intended to disguise her growing anxiety.

"What? My San Diego bride fears a bit of fog?" he teased, chuckling.

When she didn't respond, he added, "We're almost there, my dove. Never fear. I can see the road well enough if I keep my speed down. I've driven here many times."

Linnea inhaled and attempted to relax into the soft leather of the bucket seat. She pushed a button. Soon, comforting warmth embraced her. Despite herself, she still felt elated with Mehmet's luxury SUV and all its pleasures. It wasn't so long ago that she'd been jolting around town in her little VW rust bucket, reliable and good on gas but not a glamour queen. It certainly didn't compare to the vehicles her new husband owned.

Mehmet clicked the satellite radio and the soothing rhythm of *Clair de lune* coaxed tension from her shoulders.

The fog lights reflected back, the area more than a few feet beyond the hood a mystery. A tilt of her head against the rest and she watched mist whisk over and around the rear-view outside her window.

Dark fog splattered against her window. She gasped and jerked away. Again. Black fog. Was it smoke? *What the hell is it?* Lillianna wondered. Cobalt grey swirls spun so fast she feared they'd crack the glass and leaned further away. The gold signal light below the mirror flickered, grew brighter, and she blinked to reassure herself she hadn't seen eyes glaring straight at her as Mehmet turned the vehicle right.

"Linnea, what's wrong?"

"There's....I saw....something's not right. There's something out there."

"Nothing but sand and stone. I swear. Try to relax. I thought you would feel more comfortable being alone together on the first drive to the house, but perhaps I should have had Omer, my driver, pick us up. You must be so exhausted. I should have insisted we stay overnight in Istanbul before going to your new home." A screech and hiss sounded from the back. "It seems Sabrina has had enough of travel too," he added.

"Oh, my poor baby. We'll be there soon, my little sweetie. Can you imagine if she'd had to travel in the hold of some commercial plane? I doubt she'd have made it," Linnea said. She reached into the back and gave a small tap to the top of Sabrina's carrier. The Siamese wasn't placated and meowed her dissatisfaction. "I know, sweetie. We'll be there soon."

Her words helped to soothe her as well as her pet.

She was more relieved, however, when Mehmet turned off the main road. They pulled to a stop next to an elevated keypad, and she breathed in deeply. Wrought iron gates slid away behind a high-walled enclosure and Mehmet continued down a long, palm-lined drive, each tree illuminated by high beams of landscape lighting. It reminded Linnea of a swanky resort entrance rather than a single family residence. Without fog too, she noted. A haven then.

As they pulled under a wide porte-cochere, several people streamed down the stone steps from the double doors of the massive stucco and brick structure. She gasped as her car door was drawn open. She hadn't noticed the dark suited man who must have already been standing in the shadows.

He nodded in acknowledgement. "Asani hanim," he said, gesturing for her to exit, which she quickly did. She knew Mehmet was wealthy, after all they traveled in a private jet, but the dwelling before which she now stood felt intimidating. *Will it ever feel like home*? she wondered.

When she noticed a young woman reaching for Sabrina's carrier, she said, "Wait, I'll take her. She's pretty upset."

"Of course," the woman said, stepping back and nodding.

Shouldering her purse, she reached for Sabrina and said softly, "Okay, sweetie, we're here. You'll be near a litter box and some food and water shortly." Sabrina hissed her distain, clearly not believing anything good was coming her way. Linnea wondered if she should have administered another sedative the vet provided and she decided was too risky and unnecessary.

She trotted up the steps and asked the young woman who followed, garment and carryon bags in hand, "Can you show me where Sabrina's amenities have been set up?"

"This way, please," the woman said, heading across marble floors that gleamed under the light of an impressive chandelier, toward the winding great staircase constructed of marble and iron that curved up the right side of the vaulted foyer.

Linnea saw Mehmet on the phone yet again and followed with Sabrina. "I'm so sorry. I should have introduced myself."

"All here know of you and your recent marriage, Asani hanim. My name is Fatima. I will be your personal maid. You will meet the rest of the staff after you have settled your sacred cargo. You must be famished as well as tired. Cook prepared refreshment."

"That sounds wonderful," Linnea said. "I am drained, but I'm also starving and would love to get something into my stomach before bedtime." She glanced over the railing and sighed. She hoped Mehmet would be true to his word and actually have a honeymoon. Moving into her new home was a cinch since she'd been told all her belongings had already arrived and been put away.

Time would tell.

So far Mehmet spent more time with his phone than with her.

***

Mehmet snored softly beside her, Sabrina lay on top of the covers, snugged against her foot, and

Linnea glanced around the room, wondering what had awoken her, then briefly where she was until she remembered. New home, new sounds. Hell, new country, people, language, customs, not for adventure, for good. Stress might have been a big reason why it was 2 a.m. according to the illuminated clock on the nightstand beyond the canopied bedcurtains and she was wide awake.

And now so was Sabrina. The Siamese stretched and arched her back, licked her foot, then suddenly sprang from the bed and ran toward the corner as though something caught her attention. Linnea watched the feline's shadow cast from the light of the dimmed wall sconces.

The cat sat immobile, transfixed upon the something fifteen feet above its head in the corner. Linnea looked up and studied the deep shadows that drew her pet's attention but could see nothing to account for Sabrina's rapt stare.

Perhaps a spider or insect of some kind, she speculated, hoping it wasn't the former, or worse yet, a scorpion. That thought brought her to her feet and she hurried forward, not wanting her sweet kitty to get stung. As she neared the corner, a dark shadow appeared to move. To move. The cat's attention moved with it.

Now Linnea stared, trying to decide what she had seen. Had she seen anything? Another movement, then another, faster, and she watched with disbelief as the shadows undulated across the edge of the ceiling until they seemed to settle, darker, malevolent, into the far corner. The cat, having followed the entire distance of the wall, stared a moment and then seemed to lose interest as if whatever had been was no more.

If it had been at all.

The next morning, Mehmet took her shopping and sightseeing in Istanbul, spending the entire day with her, letting her help him choose some new suits at his tailor's, after which he insisted on helping her choose dresses, and even surprised her with gold bangles he claimed all dignified married ladies in Istanbul must wear or it would be thought their husband didn't adore and worship them, as he claimed to fervently adore her. She laughed and they dined and she forgot to mention the shadows.

That night he demonstrated his love and they both slept soundly.

After a day in town, they spent a day lazing around the pool and making love in the middle of the day, as honeymooners are apt to do. He took only 2 calls during lunch, and then told her regrettably he would have to join a quick video conference after dinner.

She decided to take a bath. The deeply sunken tub with its bottles of fragrant oils and foaming scents called to her.

When she reached the bathroom what she noticed first were the scents of jasmine and sandalwood. Steam rose between the bubbles in the tub. Someone had overheard her remarks at dinner and informed her maid. Fluffy towels soaked up warmth from the heater beside the marble tub. Of equal allure were the dozen candles scattered around the room.

Linnea got naked and submerged in under a minute.

Leaned back on a foam pillow she chuckled as Sabrina swatted at the mountain of bubbles near the side of the tub, a habit she started as a kitten and still enjoyed. "Oh, Sabrina, didn't I sneak you enough fish tidbits at dinner? You won't have so much fun if you fall in."

The feline swatted a few more times, tired of her game, and jumped down. Linnea's eyes slid shut and she sighed with utter contentment. She enjoyed her honeymoon now that Mehmet managed to make room in his schedule for her.

Soon enough, she would be back to work herself, chronicling her joy of Istanbul for the travel magazine for which she worked. One of the things that made her and Mehmet perfect for each other were his frequent business trips all over the world, and her ability to accompany him and busy herself with sightseeing while he conducted less interesting, although clearly more profitable, business of his own.

She opened her eyes long enough to grasp the sea sponge on the shelf beside the tub and dunked it, bringing it up to squeeze hot water onto her shoulders.

Sabrina screeched and snarled, sounding as though she fought in an alley. Linnea stood and snatched a towel as she stepped from the tub and rushed, slipping once on the wet marble, toward the bedroom. The sound stopped as she arrived, her pet nowhere to be seen. "Sabrina? Where are you kitty? Come here, come back. Where did you go, sweetie?"

Linnea quickly dried, donned her robe and searched the bedroom, under the bed, in the closets, behind the settee and the end tables. She enlisted the maid, the cook, the butler and the housekeeper. After his meeting, she enlisted Mehmet. They all searched.

Sabrina's name sounded over the entire mansion.

Sabrina was not found. Not that day, not the next, and not the day after that.

A wide-brim hat shielded her from the hot sun and Linnea called, "Sabrina! Sabrina!" and walked further along the rocky terrain. She heard a motor coming toward her and leaned against a rock outcropping to wipe her brow and wait for the vehicle to pass. It didn't pass, however. It stopped when it reached her.

"Asani hanim, your husband has obtained this vehicle for your use in searching for your sacred cat," Amid called, loud enough to be heard over the vehicle's engine. "Please allow me to escort you."

She got in without argument, actually thankful for the ride in what looked like a cross between a dune buggy and a Humvee, complete with heavy duty roll bars and complicated seat belts. The latter, Amid, her driver Mehmet had informed her yesterday, helped her fasten. He then handed her a bottle of water, which she also accepted with gratitude. She wasn't yet used to all the help and attention her husband's staff afforded her but couldn't deny it was comforting right now.

Sabrina had never run away before. Linnea wondered if the long journey had caused her too much anxiety. She was used to traveling with Linnea on short trips, but on trips this far from home she usually stayed with a neighbor, Ellie, a good friend and fellow feline lover. Sabrina loved Ellie, who was a frequent visitor and treat bringer to Linnea's condo in San Diego. The condo was now gone, but the friendship remained. Ellie had expressed empathy and emotional support Linnea needed just that morning--support Linnea needed because Mehmet had to return to Istanbul and work today.

Hours later, she agreed with Amid that they would have to go out again the next morning as it was getting too dark to see well on the rough and potentially dangerous terrain. Mehmet would be home soon, too.

She went upstairs as soon as they returned, ready to shower off the dust and discouragement of another unsuccessful day. Raising her arm to toss her hat on the bed, she froze. Sabrina lay sleeping, curled up on her pillow, oblivious to the stir she caused.

"Sabrina!" Linnea called and ran to the bed. The cat, clearly startled and not too pleased to be so rudely awoken, meowed in protest and sprang from the bed just as Linnea reached for her. She sat on the floor licking her foot. "Oh, Sabrina. Where have you been, you silly beast? I've been searching for four days, and here you are calmly bathing."

To her credit, the feline did look up and tilt her head, staring at Linnea with big, innocent blue eyes.

"You found her? That's wonderful," Fatima said from the open doorway. "I will alert the rest of the staff and have fresh food set out. Where did you find her?"

"I thought you might have found her," Linnea said, stooping to snatch the culprit up into a hug and snug. The feline had the good sense to purr loudly and rub her face against her devoted mistress's.

"No one has seen her in four days. I thought you must have found her on your search today."

"The little minx was sleeping on my pillow when I walked in. I wonder where she could have been? Well, she looks none the worse for her adventures." Just to be sure, she lifted the cat and gave her a thorough once-over. "Well, I'm taking a shower and she's staying in the room with me behind closed doors the entire time," Linnea announced and headed for the bathroom, feline firmly captured in her arms.

***

Sabrina had been back for two days now, the first of which Linnea kept her in sight by closing each room she entered after making sure her pet was inside. The second day, she began to notice that the normally independent cat was never more than a few feet away from her, most often sitting in her lap or on the arm of her chair. If she left the house, the cat was sitting at the door awaiting her entrance.

Coming in from the pool, Linnea picked Sabrina up and said, "What is it, sweetie? Did you get lost and scared you'd never see me again? Don't worry, everyone knows to keep the downstairs windows and doors closed at all times. You won't slip out again. You're safe now, sweetie." Apparently comforted, the cat purred loudly and rubbed her cheek against Linnea's.

She carried her furry companion upstairs with her, sitting her down as she prepared for a shower.

She was pleased but a little surprised to find the cat calmly sitting outside the shower when she emerged a few minutes later. The feline never took her eyes off her these days. *She really is afraid*, Linnea thought. She would have to ask Fatima to sit with her and give her treats and her kitty toys when Amid drove her into town to meet Mehmet for dinner.

"I wonder if I should take Sabrina to the vet," Linnea said across the table to her husband who was tasting the wine.

He swallowed and said, "It shall be as you wish, my flower, but the cat seems perfectly healthy to me." He nodded for the waiter to pour. "If it will ease your worry, I'll have Amid take you tomorrow. Sultan will know where to go and make the arrangements."

"Thank you, Mehmet. It would make me feel better."

The housekeeper made the arrangements and the vet was seen. He proclaimed Sabrina fit as a fiddle and it made Linnea feel better, for a day.

But she awoke that night to find Sabrina sitting on her pillow beside her head, staring. Staring at her. Watching her breath. Once she realized Linnea was awake, the feline moved closer and rubbed her check against Linnea's face. For some reason, it felt possessive in an unnatural, an eerie sort of way.

Linnea sat up. The cat moved behind her and began rubbing against her back. Linnea got out of bed. She turned to look at the feline, who walked to the edge of the bed as if to see where her mistress would go next.

So she could follow.

"Are you a guard cat now?" Linnea asked, but she didn't chuckle. Her brows pulled downward with the disturbing thoughts that came to her mind. *Is Sabrina indeed guarding me, or stalking me? Like prey.*

She threw her heavy blond tussle of bedhead curls over her shoulder and headed for the bathroom. A turn of her head wasn't necessary to know the cat followed her, but she glanced back anyway. The Siamese tread in her footsteps.

"Don't you have to go to the bathroom or something?" she asked. "It's not necessary to be with me every second. You're acting like a service dog all of a sudden." Except a service dog wouldn't make her feel so uncomfortable. Sabrina had become her shadow.

She became even more disturbed when Fatima informed her that the cat hadn't been using its litter box or eating her food. She'd been back for several days. Where was she going to the bathroom and what was she eating? If she were going somewhere in the house they would have smelled it. The fastidious housekeeper would have found it. "What's going on with you?" she asked her ever-present companion. "What happened to you?" she asked and then wondered where such a notion came from. *Did something happen to her? But what?* she wondered.

At dinner she asked Mehmet, who looked at her in confusion, not understanding why a cat who caused her panic when missing suddenly caused her distress because she was always present. And how could she explain what she didn't understand herself?

The next morning, after Mehmet had already left for work, Linnea awoke to find Sabrina standing on her pillow with her face just above hers. Instinct made her try to move away, but to her surprise she was unable to.

Sabrina moved though. She saw a flicker of orange and red, like flames, within the depth of the cat's blue eyes before they filled with swirling cobalt darkness. The Siamese's body began to shimmer and then transform into a smokey, undulating mass.

The mass moved closer and then closer. Linnea couldn't move.

Couldn't scream.

Her mouth and nostrils were suffocated as the mass suddenly moved into her body, invading her mind. She could hear the cat, who was clearly not a cat, laughing at her helplessness as it took over her body. It took over her mind but not her will. She could feel it. She felt as if she'd been shoved into a tiny black corner of herself, an observer, no longer in control of her own body.

She was being dominated by some dark, sinister being. Screams filled her mind, or what little of it she had left. Helpless, terrified screams. No one could hear her of course.

And then the darkness consumed her.

***

"I quit my job today," the evil entity informed Mehmet.

"As you wish, my love, but I thought you loved your job."

"I want to start working with you. Surely you could use some help somewhere, with all your holdings and interests."

"With me?" He looked up from his plate, his expression surprise, but not displeasure.

"Yes, I think it would help me adapt to the culture and people better if I spent more time with them. It would certainly help me better understand why my husband is so often on his phone. We could do lunch and spend more time together."

"I wouldn't want you to get tired of me," he said, smiling.

"As if I could," the entity said, pressing her lips up into a smile.

"You would be a good fit for the marketing division," Mehmet suggested.

"I was thinking perhaps something in the financial division," the entity coaxed.

"We can speak with the CFO tomorrow, if you like," he said, placing his hand over hers. "I just want you to feel happy in your new home. I know how much you've given up coming here to start a new life with me, Linnea. I want to help you feel comfortable and I know you like to keep busy. We will find a good fit. Never fear."

But that's exactly what she did fear.

The creature let her see its plans, perhaps to torture her. To terrify her.

It worked.

It had taken possession of her a week ago. She was able to be 'awake' for longer periods of time and wondered if keeping her a prisoner in her own body was wearing the creature down, making it tired.

She tried often to struggle against it, and that night she was able to move at last. Though she wanted to wake Mehmet and tell him what happened, she didn't dare. What could she say that wouldn't make her sound crazy? What proof did she have? She still looked the same, but just when she tried to get control the entity would awaken and shove her back into that tiny space in her mind where she could see and hear but do nothing to prevent the diabolical plans the creature had for her husband and his billions.

Though Sabrina was back, she no longer stalked her and in fact seemed to avoid her and hissed whenever she came near. The cat, for at last that's what she truly was, knew there was an intruder in her mistress's body.

But no one else seemed to notice, which actually infuriated Linnea. Not that it mattered. She couldn't do anything about it.

Not yet.

Realizing the entity must be resting, asleep perhaps, she got out of bed and went to the study. She remembered something she learned about when she traveled in Egypt. She thought it was just a legend then. Now she wasn't so sure.

Sitting down at the computer, she unlocked it with her birthdate and typed 'Jinn' into the search engine. She scrolled past the movie and imaginary sources and found some serious and more scholarly references. Just a few moments later her worst fears were confirmed.

A jinn possessed her.

Any attempt she made to escape her tormentor was likely to end in failure once it took her mind and body over again.

It was true.

She knew it.

Even as she sat there and searched for a solution, someone to help her, she doubted they could. Still she sought until she found the contact information of an imam known for his academic wisdom and study of the old texts, the old ways. He, she felt sure, would know, and understand. And help. The entity stirred within her, and she pushed back with all her might.

Just a few moments more.

She sent off an email explaining her plight and why any return contact may not reach her, the real her.

Then she slept, for the jinn awakened.

***

Linnea knew the man standing at her office door was the imam she'd contacted. The jinn did not. It stood and motioned the man to a chair, nodding.

"Hosgeldin. To what do I owe this honor, Imam?"

He studied her silently a moment and she wondered if he saw a stray fleck of burning fire within the depth of her green eyes, the true sign of a jinn presence.

"Hoşbuldum. I felt I needed to come in person to thank you for such a generous donation, Asani hanim."

"That was not necessary at all. Would you like tea?" the entity asked, gracious to a fault.

As the creature spoke, it gestured to the young assistant entering with tea for two.

"You do me honor, Asani hanim." He turned his attention to the assistant and said, "Two sugars if you please."

Linnea watched with fascination as the imam continued the nonsense banter. He watched the creature that controlled her body by dominating the greatest portion of her mind.

She pushed against the trap in her mind continuously, but the entity pushed back just as hard. Harder. She was able to escape for brief periods of time, but not now, not when she really needed to.

Help! I'm in here. Do an exorcism or something! is what she wanted to say.

"Leaving so soon, Imam?" is what that creature made her say.

Pleasantries over, the imam left, her hopes with him.

Over lunch, Mehmet informed the ever charming and loving monster in her body that he had a dinner meeting tonight.

She was surprised when the jinn told Amid to drive her to the home of the CFO after work. She was especially surprised it knew where to go.

Mufasa lived in a large, brightly painted house, right on the water. He seemed to be expecting her, opening the door before she even had a chance to knock.

He not only expected her, she realized, he expected more than business from her. Or, rather, the whorish creature inside her who was accepting a drink and . . . why couldn't she stop it, herself, the demonic entity, from doing this? It pulled Mufasa's head down and kissed him passionately and Linnea wondered if she could at least make herself vomit.

"A little more ice in my drink?"

"Of course," Mufasa said and taking it moved to the bar.

Linnea watched as the jinn slipped a vial from her purse and poured its contents into the glass Mufasa had set on the end table. When Mufasa returned, he handed Linnea her drink before picking up his own and taking a large swallow.

What, she wondered, had the jinn made her give him? The brute loved to push her into unawareness whenever it wanted to surprise her later--a surprise she could do nothing to prevent. It loved to torture her, but now apparently it wanted to do worse.

They moved to the sofa and before long had finished their drinks. The bastard began pawing her and the damn jinn let him. Her torment was thankfully short lived. Mufasa, whose speech became increasingly slurred, rubbed at his eyes and mumbled something. His gaze looked dull and his expression confused before he slumped over.

The jinn poisoned him? What could she do? Linnea tried to force her way out of her imprisonment. The jinn, either because it sensed her helpless panic or because it's poison had worked, laughed.

It then went into the bedroom and into the back of the closet and opened the safe. Linnea wondered how she knew the location or combination, or rather, how the jinn knew. But it wasn't robbing the safe.

A gun?

What was it going to do with a gun?

What was it going to make her do with a gun?

It returned to the sofa, to the apparently not yet dead Mufasa and after carefully wiping off her fingerprints from the gun, placed it in Mufasa's hand. Then, remembering that the CFO was left-handed, removed it, wiped it clean again, and put the gun in his left hand. Raising the gun to his temple, it used Mufasa's finger to pull the trigger.

Linnea screamed, though only laughter emerged from her mouth. She tried desperately to squeeze her eyes shut, to not see the blood ooze from the blackish hole in the side of Mufasa's temple. Instead, she reached for both glasses and took them to the kitchen where she carefully washed and dried them before returning them to the bar.

Picking up her purse, the jinn withdrew a handwritten note and placed it on the table. Then she walked to the door, locked and closed it, and met Amid on his way up the walk.

"I thought I heard something. Are you okay?"

"Everything is as it should be," the jinn said, continuing to the car.

Amid hurried forward to open the door for her.

The next morning, at the office, the jinn showed Mehmet some ledgers and accused Mufasa of embezzling. Mehmet found it difficult to believe until the police arrived and revealed Mufasa's apparent suicide. He left a note, expressing his deep remorse for his transgressions. When asked what transgressions the man might have been ashamed of, Mehmet informed the police that he was shocked and had no idea that Mufasa had any problems at all.

Later that evening, Mehmet turned her in his arms and gently cupping her chin to tilt her head back. "Did you kill Mufasa, Linnea? Did you perhaps confront him and kill him in self-defense for what he did at the company? Amid told me you were there and he thought he heard a gunshot."

"Don't worry, my love. I have already taken care of the damage Mufasa caused, and transferred the funds back into the company accounts, removed all trace of the accounts Mufasa opened in his own name. The police will find nothing. I could easily take over his position to be sure this never happens again, if you like."

Mehmet stood still and silent a moment, looking into her eyes and no doubt considering what the jinn left unsaid, what it meant, and what the consequences might be. Then, softly, he said, "I'm sure you will keep our company safe, and I will protect you from any who would try to harm you. Ever. Amid is trusted and loyal. He will say nothing."

The jinn smiled.

It then did things with and to Mehmet that Linnea had never tried, never wanted to try.

The next day she awoke bruised, the purpling marks on her body a testament to the rough play the jinn had encouraged and expressed ecstasy over the night before. The beast smiled back at her in the mirror, mockingly, fiery sparks shining from the depth of her eyes.

Linnea shuddered inwardly, and then dressed and joined Mehmet for breakfast. It kissed him lovingly, touching his hand, making the anxious look of inquiry at her well-being change to adoration.

Her life continued in much the same way until one night the jinn told her in the bathroom mirror, "I like this luscious body, Linnea. I can see why Mehmet adores it. You. I like what Mehmet can do to it, the pleasure it affords him."

Which is why Linnea felt surprise and confusion when the jinn exchanged a loving kiss with her husband and then rolled over as if to sleep. Relieved, Linnea slept, thankful for the respite.

Her surprise continued when she awoke the next day to realize she was not only in control of her body, but alone in her body and mind, the jinn gone. Sabrina jumped on the bed and purred loudly, rubbing her cheek against Linnea's. Even the cat knew she was back.

Mehmet walked in from the bathroom, toweling off his dark, shoulder-length hair, another towel wrapped around his waist. Linnea sprang from the bed and hurried toward him only to stop when Sabrina hissed and snarled at him before running from the room.

"I wonder why your cat hates me so?" he said. Linnea noticed the orange glints flare in the depth of his dove gray eyes and groaned.

He reached out to caress her and she flinched away.

Chuckling, he said, "Oh, I have so much more I will teach you, my dearest. What fun we shall have. And let me introduce myself. My name is Bazel, my dearest bride."

When she opened her mouth to protest, he placed his finger on her lips and said, "Unless of course you would like Mehmet to walk off the roof, or perhaps use the gun from his desk drawer."

"No, wait. Please don't hurt him," she said, wiping moisture from the corners of her eyes. She wouldn't give this vile creature that pleasure.

"As you wish, so long as you . . . shall we say, cooperate?"

"Fine," she said, but what she thought was, *I'm going to find a way to defeat you.*

"Tsk, tsk, none of those ideas. I am not alone my dear and could easily have one of my associates *make* you become more cooperative."

Could it read her mind, or was it just guessing? Either way, Linnea cringed to think of being invaded by yet another jinn, perhaps even more perverse than this one. "I said I'll cooperate," she said.

"Good. Come here and demonstrate your cooperation," the cruel being demanded, leering wickedly and pointing toward the bed.

Linnea had no choice. At least not for now.

Several hours later, she sat at her desk and replaced the phone to its stand. It was harder than she thought to convince Ellie that all was fine and wonderful in her new home, with her new husband, while trying to block out the morning's degrading debauchery. Rubbing the ache in her temples, she glanced up and gasped. Standing in her doorway was an unannounced visitor.

The imam studied her closely, then walked forward and held out an item which she took and studied. A relic of some kind.

She looked up, brows knit. "What is this for?"

"A test. A jinn could never dare to touch this sacred relic that once belonged to King Solomon. It's nice to finally meet you, Asani hanim."

"Thank you. I'm happy to be free of him, but he's now in Mehmet and I can't move against him or he has threatened to kill my husband and have my body repossessed by another jinn."

The white-bearded man nodded. "I see. Well, I never said it would be easy. Are you willing to risk dying to try?"

Thinking back to the morning, Linnea said firmly, "Yes, what can I do?"

"The first thing you must do is learn absolute secrecy. You must convince the jinn that he has won, that you are terrified of what he might do. This means you must do whatever he demands. Are you ready and willing to do that?"

"That much I have already done. But I won't do anything that endangers Mehmet."

The imam nodded. "Here," he said, handing her a card. "Go here during your lunch. Let no one know."

She read the business card with some surprise. It was a dovme salonu, a tattoo parlor. When she looked up to question him, the imam was already disappearing out the door.

She went to lunch with Mehmet, at his command, or rather Bazel's, and pleasured him in the back of the car before they entered the restaurant. She felt thankful he at least had Omer leave the car and stand on the sidewalk beforehand, and that the windows were darkly tinted. She told herself the body was that of her husband, to keep from retching.

After lunch, which she had with Mehmet, or rather Bazel, she went back to the office, then hailed a taxi. She handed the driver the card to read the address, then settled back to observe the changing scenery. They left the busy financial district and headed toward the outskirts, down bumpier, less manicured roads. The streets became narrower, the buildings in disrepair.

The driver stopped at a dingy brick building with Turkish lettering that matched the card she'd been given. She paid the driver and cautiously approached the door. It swung open on well-oiled hinges, and she walked across the large room to a counter with tubes of ointments and displays of jewelry for various piercings. Dozens of posters with grids of design patterns covered the walls. Down the left wall were numerous curtained cubicles. One was open and she saw a black vinyl chair that looked like it could recline. A table beside it held various tools and the walls there, too, were covered with dozens of designs.

"Hosgeldin," said a young woman at the counter.

"I was sent here by the imam," Linnea said.

She saw surprise register on the woman's face before she nodded and gestured toward the door at the rear of the room, beyond the counter.

Swallowing, Linnea summoned her courage and walked with more confidence than she felt to the door. Wondering if she should knock, she hesitated only to have the door opened.

"You came," the imam said.

"Yes, though I'm not sure why you had me meet you here."

"All will be revealed shortly. Come with me."

He led her to a table at the end of the small room and switched on a light. A middle-aged man, heavily tattooed, walked to the table and set down a jar of black ink and a tattoo tool. Walking to a small cabinet, he returned with an electric razor which he plugged into the wall beside the table.

"Sit here please," the imam said.

"No. Wait. What are you going to do?" Linnea asked.

"I can imagine your fear. I am going to put a sacred symbol upon your body in the only place we can hope to hide it. The intent is to prevent your body and mind from being possessed again. We don't want to risk the jinn's anger by letting him detect it, so the best place of concealment seems within your hair. We need to shave a tiny area in order to apply the tattoo and the hair will grow back over it to conceal it completely. Your only risk is while it heals and before the hair grows back in again, so you will have to wear your hair down or done up over the area. That's why here," he pointed out, touching a place at the back of her head about 4 inches above the hairline at her neck, "seems the best place."

"How big is small?" Linnea asked. She knew what it felt like because she had a tiny dragonfly on her right shoulder.

"This size," the imam said, holding out a small sheet filled with various symbols. Each one was only about an inch tall and half an inch wide. "This one," he said, pointing to a design in the middle.

"The hand of Fatima?" Linnea asked, recognizing the common symbol. "Can't I just wear a necklace? I think I have one, in fact."

"You will do both. Here," he said, handing her an intricate filigree sphere covered by a dark blue enamel. It hung from a long, golden chain. "The symbol is inside, where it can't be seen, protected from the jinn by lead, which is poisonous to them. It is toxic to humans to a lesser degree, which is why it's covered with enamel, to protect you from the toxin. The jinni will sense the lead and avoid contact, but may demand you remove it, which is why you must also wear a symbol hidden on your person."

"What if he finds the tattoo?"

"Then you will be in great danger, I fear. The choice is yours, but it will prevent you from being repossessed, which seemed a great concern to you."

Linnea considered a moment. Then, remembering what it felt like to be possessed, how the jinn could make her do whatever it wanted, she nodded and took a seat.

***

It was several days before the jinn noticed her necklace. Thankfully, it had not yet noticed the tattoo.

"You have worn that before. I don't really care for it. Take it off," Mehmet, or rather the jinn, commanded.

"But my best friend gave it to me before I left America. I wear it all the time."

He folded his arms and glared.

She took it off and put it into her jewelry box.

"Now take off your clothes."

She took a slow deep breath and did as he ordered.

"Come here. Hold out your hands."

She complied, reluctantly, wondering if he would swat her hands with a switch like her 4th grade teacher had once done.

A gasp escaped her when he snapped handcuffs on her before she could resist. He quickly laced a rope through the space between them and tossed it over the top rail of the canopy bed. He pulled until she was on tiptoe before securing the rope.

"What are you doing?" she protested.

"Whatever I want. Now shut up," he said, shoving a ball into her mouth that was attached to a string which he tied around her head, securing it at her neck, thankfully, so the not quite healed tattoo wasn't disturbed or revealed.

Her thankfulness didn't last long. He grabbed her hair and tossed it over her shoulder.

"Stop this," she screamed through her gag, although all that came out was a muffled murmur, which served to make her choke and do as he'd ordered so she could breathe through her nose. The suffocating feel of the thing in her mouth made her panic. She struggled against the rope that secured her, making the metal railing over her head rattle.

He twisted her around and slapped her in the face. Not hard enough to bruise, but hard enough to make her stop, and hard enough to bring tears to her eyes.

With another jerk, he turned her around again and walked away a moment. She relaxed a little, trying to slow her breathing, hoping her punishment was to just be left hanging here on her tiptoes for a while.

She was wrong.

She heard his bare footsteps behind her before she felt the pain or heard the slap of the flogger on her buttocks. Shocked, she sucked in her breath. Not satisfied with her response, he hit her again, harder. Screaming, she pulled against her restraints and puffed in and out of her nose, trying to breathe through her discomfort. She no sooner settled herself than Mehmet struck her again, and then again and again.

Tears streamed down her face and her nose started to run. She blew it out, not caring what she looked like, just trying not to suffocate. *Clearly the bastard wants to beat me to death*, she thought as another blow struck her, this time on her other butt cheek. She strained away, unable to escape the burning agony. *Do people actually like this?* she wondered. *How could they? God, make him stop.*

Linnea lost track of how many times he struck her, chuckling each time she screamed beneath the gag. Ten minutes? Twenty? Her ass and her thighs burned, and her calves burned and started to cramp from being on her toes, which also hurt. Her wrists hurt, though the cuffs were lined with some cushioning material. And her arms ached from trying to hold her hands up to relieve the pressure on her wrists—which were punished each time a blow fell and she instinctively jerked away from it.

Then he stopped and she heard him walk away, toward the dresser. She listened intently, afraid of what new terror he would conjure. He was soon back and her worst fears were realized. She screamed. She chocked. His previous beatings were just a warmup. Whatever flogger he now used it stung. It stung and burned and even sounded louder. It hurt more if that were possible.

It was.

Linnea's right butt cheek felt numb, though she could still feel the burning sensation every time he flogged her. Her mind couldn't seem to keep up with the sensations. For a moment, she thought she might actually like it, but then reasoned it must be some Stockholm Syndrome thing. She hated Bazel and hated pain. Why did the next blow make her feel . . . how did it make her feel?

She stopped responding as she struggled to understand her reaction to this torture. Her momentary response revolted her. She felt guilty, ashamed.

She had long since given up trying to plead through the gag. It just excited the animal inside her husband. Her husband. They had never even discussed such things as spankings and floggings and handcuffs and bondage, nothing BDSM. This was madness.

Then, suddenly, the jinn spun her around and struck her on first one breast and then the other. She strained away, repulsed, horrified, crying uncontrollably.

Satisfied that she'd learned whatever lesson he was trying to teach her, the monster reached up and untied her gag, tossing it to the floor. Then, he loosed the rope and twisted a key in the cuffs. She collapsed to the floor.

"No, not quite yet pet. We're on our honeymoon, remember?"

"No - "

"Didn't I just explain that you're to do whatever I say the moment I say so, without argument or explanation?" He chuckled and added, "And that you're to enjoy doing so?"

Dammit. Did he know the conflict and confusion within her? Damn him! He was angry that she didn't immediately take the necklace off without talking back, Linnea realized. But did he also want to bend her to this perversion, for perversion it must surely be. Had his possession of her left a trace of his vile nature within her, hidden away in a small dark place like the one he'd forced her to live in while he dominated her, from within?

He snapped the flogger against his hand to get her attention.

She jumped. "What do you want me to do?"

"That's better. Now get in bed and I'll make it up as I go." He tossed her a box of tissue. Stop crying. You're a mess. Get in bed. Now! I want to mess you up some more."

He laughed at her quick response.

"Much better," he said.

She spent another hour doing exactly as the vile bastard wanted, anything to avoid more beatings, and then Linnea escaped to the bathroom where she sat on the floor of the shower and cried until the water grew too cold to bear.

***

"I don't know if I can go on, Iman."

"The choice is yours. Do you think you can make him follow you?"

"Yes, I think he will if his ego is tested. He's incredibly arrogant."

"Then everything is in place. You need only lure him to the building. Do you think he suspects duplicity?"

"After last night, I think he suspects abject obedience."

"Did something happen, child?" the imam said, his empathy clear in his dark amber gaze.

"I'd rather not talk about it," she said, the pain from her humiliation still burning and her bruised flesh reminder enough. "Can we do this today? Can I get rid of him and get my husband back today?"

"If you feel strong enough."

Linnea took a long drink of the hot tea and set the glass down. It rattled in the saucer due to her shaking hands.

"You're sure?" the imam asked again.

"What time?"

"3 o'clock."

"I'll bring him then," she said softly.

He simply nodded and hurried off to check on the preparations.

Linnea took a folder of files to Mehmet's office. He was in conversation with his assistant who Linnea realized would need to be fired soon as it seemed apparent her husband's captor was having an affair with the young female. She looked guilty as hell when she saw Linnea standing in the doorway.

Mehmet, or rather Bazel, smiled and said, "Ah, my bride, how wonderful to see you, and so soon after lunch. I'm sorry I wasn't able to join you today." He looked pointedly at the assistant and chuckled.

The woman mumbled an excuse and fled.

Linnea wished she could join her.

"Good to see you keeping so fit, husband," she said sarcastically.

He raised a brow and looked her up and down as though examining a prize mare.

She felt dirty.

"I prefer a more gentle, perhaps even more experienced form of exercise," she taunted.

His eyes narrowed.

"I have a business meeting out of the office, so I wanted to drop off these files you requested. Don't worry, I'll be home in time for dinner," she said and dropped the files on his desk, hurrying from the room before he could detain her.

She quickly stepped into the elevator and rode it to the ground floor. She stopped in the lobby to powder her nose and check her mirror to see if he'd taken the bait and followed her.

He had.

She exited the building and hailed a taxi, again using her mirror to see that his driver pulled his car up and got out so Mehmet could drive himself. Clearly he didn't want anyone to know where he was going or what he might do when he got there.

It took just fifteen minutes to reach their destination. She glanced up and down the street to check for cars before crossing, and to make sure Mehmet hadn't lost her.

He was parked down the block.

She hurried inside and was greeted by the imam.

"This way, stand in the center of the room, directly on top of that symbol, so he sees you, with your back to the door. I'm going to prop it open."

She grabbed her forearms and shuddered. If this didn't work, she knew Bazel would kill her.

Or worse.

The imam returned and stood facing her, facing the doorway. He placed his hand upon her shoulder, head down as if they were quietly conversing.

"Your taste is diverse, my bride. I'll grant you points for variety."

He glanced back, seeing a young boy spread salt across the exit threshold. Frowning, he turned back to Linnea. "You surprise me once again, my emerald-eyed princess. You can't honestly hope to defeat me." He laughed, but she sensed his alert attention. He was not without vulnerability, and he seemed to realize that she, or the man with her, knew what they were.

He was right.

The imam rotated in a circle and poured salt around the symbol upon which they stood. Then, he drew the evil eye within the circle.

"You can't think that will keep me out, holy man. Now I see the real reason you visited Linnea's office. It seems you've returned a time or two."

The imam ignored him, and Linnea was too terrified to speak, which must have infuriated him because he stormed into the room screaming in Turkish, which meant Linnea only understood a small fraction of what he said . . . the swear words.

Given the opportunity, the young boy ran a line of salt across the entrance to the room.

Mehmet stopped. He looked down, and then up, and turned in a full circle.

"You little bitch," he snarled. He had only now realized he stood in a holy sanctum, surrounded by relics and sacred symbols he dare not touch, dare not desecrate.

The imam began chanting verses from the Quran, and then what sounded to Linnea like an ancient spell in an ancient language.

"No!" Mehmet cried, clutching his head. He glared madly at Linnea and the imam and ran at them like an enraged bull.

Before she could stop herself, Linnea stepped away, out of the sacred circle. Too late she realized her own mistake.

Mehmet grabbed her and wrapped his hands around her throat, chocking her. She struggled to breath, clawing at his hands, trying to knee him in the groin, but he was too angry, too powerful for her to escape him. Her vision began to blur and she tried to suck air through her nose to no avail.

Darkness claimed her once more.

***

Mehmet watched the vile entity murdering his wife, helpless to intervene, to save her. After all the pain and atrocities the beast had visited upon her while in his body, he doubted she would ever be able to face him again, let alone love him. But still he wanted more than anything that she should live, that she should survive this nightmare they had both been enduring.

He pushed against the intruder with all his might, with all the love he felt for Linnea, for their life together.

The imam continued to chant and then reached into his pocket and pulled out an ancient gemstone that retained a symbol carved during the reign of Solomon. He pressed it against Mehmet's forehead and the jinn instantly let go of his wife. She fell to the floor.

The imam kept chanting and Mehmet kept pushing and shoving and crowding against the beast that resided within.

Then, suddenly, the entity screamed. A dark, inky smoke erupted from Mehmet's mouth and nostrils and ears. It seeped from his tear ducts and spiraled up and over his head.

The imam held the stone aloft and chanted. Young men entered the room and formed a large circle around the occupants. They carried burners of sacred incense and swung them gently side to side, picking up the imam's chant and drawing closer, pulling the circle tighter.

The black smoke swirled and darted first one way and then another, seeking an exit, an escape route.

There was none.

Mehmet looked up at the jinn to be sure it was free of him and raced to his wife's prone form. He shook her. "Linnea. Linnea, my flower, my love, please wake up."

He shook her shoulder and watched as smoke spun into a cone-like sphere and landed on the floor a short distance away. The jinn revealed its true form. A human-like form with coal-like blackness that seemed to swirl and surge and revealed brief glimpses of the orange and red and blue and yellow fires that raged within.

Moving forward, the men continued their chant. Their holy incense filled the round room. They circled the jinn. The imam held out his hands and again spoke ancient words in an ancient tongue. He placed a lead vessel on the floor, over the symbol.

The jinn screamed in agony and erupted into flames and then blue smoke that sputtered and vanished into the vessel. The imam quickly sealed the vessel with a tight-fitting lid that bore the same symbol upon which he stood.

"Is it dead?" Mehmet asked.

"Vanquished," the imam said as he moved toward the couple. He reached down and pressed the ancient talisman onto Linnea's forehead and murmured a prayer for her return to the realm and time of those living.

Linnea opened her eyes. She looked at Mehmet. He reached out his hand to cup her cheek.

She flinched away and screamed.

***

Six months had passed since the jinn's conquest and Linnea no longer woke in a cold sweat, no longer cringed at Mehmet's touch. She knew he understood, but still felt guilty when she remembered the hurt and dismay in his eyes the first time he'd tried to touch her. If nothing else she was glad she didn't have to explain to him what happened to her after the jinn left her body. He had seen it all, living the horror of it along with her, though admittedly not quite as traumatically.

He didn't know, however, how she felt about it, or the doubts and uncertainty she struggled with, thinking she might have found pleasure with their captor. It had taken more than a week with a therapist to feel comfortable letting Mehmet touch her.

Mehmet's lovemaking was gentle and sweet, and their passion most often led by her. For now. She knew he was testing her limits, her desires, not wanting to frighten or harm her.

She no longer worked for Mehmet's company, or the travel agency either. He had a new, male assistant. She was writing a book about jinn. She'd been researching them since they defeated Bazel. Who better? Her therapist agreed that it seemed to be a purging for her, as well as making her feel well-armed against them. She'd learned about flogging too, and how it released endorphins and adrenaline which produced a state of euphoria. Chemistry, not betrayal, had been her downfall.

Of course, Mehmet now knew about her secret protection, the tattoo no longer visible beneath her thick hair. She convinced him to get one on his chest, over his heart. The hair grew back over that one, too, though she could still see it faintly.

Mehmet walked into the library and bent to kiss her brow before handing her a tea and setting on the sofa beside her to drink his. He no longer hesitated before kissing her, which pleased them both.

She glanced over at him and smiled. Reaching to place his hand on her rounded stomach, he said, "How have my beautiful doves been today?"

"A good day, my love," she said sweetly.

She noticed the book open on the couch beside her and quickly closed it. It wouldn't do to have Mehmet see the chapter about jinn and propagation. He'd been through enough.

$\mathcal{R}$esurrection

Darren Simon

Under a winter's night sky fending off thick gray clouds from the east, a coyote's mournful howl and the crackle of the tiny campfire interrupted the silence of the old-world hills. A large full moon cast its yellow glow against the silver tipped Rockies towering behind the two men huddled around the dancing flame. The stench of burnt beans, black coffee and spent tobacco hovered over the two. A third member of their party, chained to an oak, shivered just beyond the fire's reach.

Three weary horses, a painted steed, a ginger and a glimmering white stallion, brazenly inched as close to the blaze as possible, seeking warmth from the evening chill.

"Any way you could see yourself to rollin' me a bit of that tobacco, Marshal Tuck? Sure would be good of you seein' how you be takin' me to hang and all." The chained man extended his shackled hands, his fingers interlocked as if in prayer. A smile crossed his grimy bone-thin face, revealing a mouth full of brown teeth. A mist drifted from his nostrils.

Marshal Tuck stared coldly at the man from underneath his wide-brimmed hat. The fingers of one hand tapped the ivory handle of his .45 nestled inside the holster of his cartridge belt. He took a long drag on the short-stemmed pipe held loosely on the right side of his dried, cracked lips. Black smoke slid out from the left slide.

For the most part, he ignored the chained man.

The second man by the fire kicked Marshal Tuck's leg with a muddy boot. "Oh, go on ya' old goat. Ain't no harm in sharin' a smoke. This one we'll be dead in the ground once we reach Yuma. Don't be stingy."

The chained man nodded. "Listen to Marshal Whitman. It's a cold night, and I'll be swingin' from a noose soon enough. Those bastards at the territorial prison... they be itchin' to string me up. Least you could do is give me a smoke tonight."

Marshal Tuck glared at his partner, then at the chained man. They'd tracked Jimmy Pierce for weeks, finally cornering him in the snow country. Pierce was wanted back in Arizona for killin' three during a bank robbery. One was a lawman. No, he'd be getting' no extra comforts on this long journey back, especially since Marshal Tuck's old bones ached in the cold. And the only reason he was here was because of this piece of trash. He cringed at the jolts of pain stretching from his shoulder blades down his back.

RESURRECTION

"Shut up, scum." Marshal Tuck's words crept from between his lips, just above a whisper—just loud enough for the others to hear. He lowered his hat over his hazel eyes and pulled his rough animal hide jacket tighter around his chest. He buried his gloved hands inside his heavy trousers. "I'm goin' to get some sleep. Bill, you take first watch. And you ever kick me again, I'll cut off your leg."

"Yeah, sure." Marshal Bill Whitman, fifteen years Marshal Tuck's junior, studied his older partner. They'd ridden long enough together to not take his threats too seriously. Sam Tuck was an ornery son of a bitch who'd threatened his life at least once every time they rode together. But Sam was a good man. An honorable man. He might be 65. The lines in his leathery forehead and under his eyes deep. His gun-slinging reflexes slowed a bit. But there was no one better on a hunt for a desperado on the run.

Pierce rattled his chains. "How about it, Marshal Whitman? Can you spare a little tobacco?"

Marshal Whitman lifted his black, scuffed hat and rubbed his gloved hands through his thick brown hair. His curly beard hid his smile. But the slight cracks on either side of his eyes gave away his amusement. "Sorry, Jimmy. You heard the man. When he's in a mood, you best not cross his orders. So just shut your mouth and get some sleep. We've got a long ride in the mornin'."

Pierce kicked his booted foot against the ground. His cheeks burned with sudden rage. "I swear I'll kill you both if I be getting' the chance. I suggest you stay awake tonight. Otherwise, it could be the death of you—if you know what I mean."

Marshal Whitman scrambled to his feet, grabbing his old Winchester. He aimed the long barrel at Pierce's head. He no longer grinned. His chest heaved. The veins in his neck, covered by a red scarf, bulged. "That sounded like a threat, friend. And I don't take kindly to threats."

Cringing, Pierce turned away from the rifle. The same weapon with droplets of his dried blood where cowardly Marshal Whitman cracked him in the head from behind. The only way these two lawmen could have caught him. Sneak up when his trousers were down takin' a shit. "Oh, I meant nothin' by it, Marshal. Didn't mean to rile you."

Marshal Tuck cleared his throat. "Tryin' to sleep here."

Marshal Whitman slowly lowered his weapon and crouched by the fire. He shouldn't let Jimmy Pierce get in his head. Sam would probably scold him on that later. *Damnit, I know better.* He hugged the

RESURRECTION

Winchester to his chest and eased his back against a hard, bumpy log.

Pierce cursed under his breath. He lifted his shackled hands to his mouth and blew on his icy fingers. The Marshals had taken his gloves. At least they let him keep his warm buckskin jacket. The one his wife sewed for him so long ago.

A coyote, maybe the same one, howled. This time, the beast sounded closer. Pierce gazed at the night sky, a patchwork of heavy, dark clouds passed over the moon, blocking its glow. The land was cast in shadowy gloom. Pierce shuddered. He cursed again. Despite the chill, fire spread through his veins.

How the hell had he let this happen? He'd been a goddamned farmer. A good one, too. It was the damn drought. He'd lost everything. He bit down on his lip until he tasted the saltiness of his own blood. A bit of the warm liquid dripped down his chin. That damned drought. No crops. Nothing to sell. He needed to feed his wife and daughter. That's the only reason he robbed that bank.

If only they'd let him walk out of there with a few measly dollars. But no, that young deputy had to get in the way. No one had to die. No one. But three did. That raw lawman and two other fools who thought they could use a gun. And now he'd hang without ever seein' his daughter or wife again.

He blinked weary eyes. His head still radiated with pain from Marshal Whitman's Winchester blow. A little tobacco would have helped ease the pain. Provide some comfort in this wilderness so far from home. Bastard Marshal Tuck. He stretched against the chain pinning him to the oak, forcing him into a sitting position, his legs spread before him. The metal links pressed against his waist. He cursed once more before closing his eyes.

Maybe if he slept, he could dream of better times with his little daughter dancin' in their wheat fields with the sun shimerin' off her golden hair. Oh, that was a site.

The horses began to neigh and shuffle their hooves. Pierce's eyes shot open. He studied them. The white stallion kicked the dirt. The painted one shifted his position to face the mountains. The ginger breathed faster, huffing loudly through its wide nostrils.

Something had them spooked.

Marshal Tuck sprang to his feet, six-shooter already freed from its holster and aimed into the blackness of the vast fields, extending to the closest mountain range. His own nostrils flared. He raised his hat higher on his forehead. His eyes stared into the darkness. His groggy brain quickly sharpened. His pulse quickened. His gun hand quivered ever so slightly. The effects of age. Not fear. He was in no mood for trouble. But he didn't fear a fight.

Marshal Whitman was immediately by his side, turning on his heels in each direction, the barrel of his Winchester out in front. The hairs on the back of his neck straightened. His muscles tightened. "What is it?"

"Somethin's movin' yonder in that direction." Marshal Tuck pointed his .45 straight ahead. He squinted his eyes. Licked his lips with a dry tongue. "Think I caught a glimpse of a horse and rider."

Pierce raised a thin eyebrow. "Uh, I'm good with a gun. Release me, throw me one, and I'll show my worth."

Both men ignored him.

Pierce shook his chains. "Shoot, I don't want to die like some dog sittin' here in the dirt. Get me up and let me fight."

"Shut up," Marshal Tuck ordered. For all he knew, whoever approached in the night was a friend of Jimmy Pierce. He'd been out here in the wilds for a few weeks. He could have formed himself a little gang.

The clouds blocking the moonlight slid away as if on cue. A soft yellow radiance once again spread over the land, casting light on a horse and rider slowly meandering across a field of green grass and tall oaks.

Marshal Tuck crept forward. His gun hand now sure and steady, no longer wavering. His finger gently brushed against the trigger. His heartbeat was deafening, blocking most other sounds, save for the rhythmic thud of the approaching horse's hooves striking the ground in a slow trot.

The stranger atop the steed was hunched over, head bobbing like a raggedy old doll.

Marshal Tuck scratched the white stubble covering his chin. *Damn. Odd. Don't like this one bit.* He pulled back the hammer on his .45, then aimed the barrel at the rider's chest. "You out there. Stop and identify yourself, else I bury a bullet in your gut."

The stranger didn't respond. The steed continued its casual stride toward them.

Marshal Whitman crossed to his older partner. He held his rifle with one hand. If need be, he could aim and fire it in less than a second. He was that good with a Winchester. One of the best. "What do you make of it?"

"Don't know, but I aim to find out." Marshal Tuck titled his head slightly and narrowed one eye. He squeezed the trigger on his weapon. A round exploded from the barrel, interrupting the night's silence with a thunderous crack.

The ground just in front of the approaching steed exploded, kicking up grass and mud.

RESURRECTION

Frightened, the horse threw its head back and reared its front legs. The mysterious rider slid off the beast, falling like a sack of potatoes onto the earth.

"Did you kill 'em, Marshal?" Pierce pressed his back against the oak, twisting his head as far as he could, but there was no way to see around the thick trunk. "Did you make sure he be good and dead? Wouldn't want you missin' and gettin' your own head blown plumb off. No sir. Wouldn't want that now."

Marshal Tuck glared in Pierce's direction.

Marshal Whitman placed a hand on Sam Tuck's shoulder. "Let me kill Jimmy now. Save us some grief."

A slight grin parted Marshal Tuck's lips. "You still good on that Winchester?"

"Have I ever given you reason to doubt me?" Marshal Whitman twisted his mustache between his fingers.

"Then cover me." Marshal Tuck started toward the rider. "I'm goin' to check on our fallen friend out there. If you see one twitch that don't look right, you fire that rifle of yours and be true with your aim." He knew there was no need to question Bill Whitman's skill with a rifle. And he trusted his partner with his life. If the stranger out there meant them harm, Bill's round would easily find its target. Still, he couldn't have his younger partner getting' too big a head for his britches.

"Sure, Sam." Marshal Whitman raised his Winchester close to his eyes. He breathed slow. Tightened his grip on the weapon. "You be careful, partner."

Marshal Tuck held his six-shooter out in front. Crossing the field, his eyes darted back and forth from the unmoving stranger to the horse that pranced around close to its fallen rider. If the rider was planning to attack, the horse would give it away. A snort. Head tilt. He knew the signs of a steed whose rider was settin' a trap.

Soft white snow began to fall around him. *Damn.* That was the last thing he needed. He'd hoped to reach the lower country before new snow fell. He hated the cold. His old bones dreaded the cold.

A frosty breeze slid through the trees, rustling leaves. The chill slapped Marshal Tuck in the face, stinging his rough cheeks. He peered skyward. Gray clouds drifted across the moon, once again blotting out its glow. The land darkened. That would make it tougher for Bill to get off a clean shot.

He pushed on, crossing the rest of the way to the fallen rider. The steed, its color raven black, backed away, the muscles in its legs twitching as if it might bolt away.

"Whoa, boy, you're okay." Marshal Tuck lifted one hand to the beast. The horse bowed its head.

Reluctantly, the horse inched closer until its snout nearly touched his hand. The steed sniffed his gloved fingers, hot steam from the nostrils seeping through cracks in the glove. "What do we have here, boy, huh? What's up with your rider?"

"Help…. Mary." The words, barely above a whisper, came from the rider. They were the words of a….

His .45 still aimed at the stranger, Marshal Tuck knelt on one knee and, with his free hand, removed the rider's hat. Staring up at him was the face of a child. A boy. Maybe no more than ten years old. The boy shivered violently. His lips parted as if to speak again but words wouldn't come.

Marshal Tuck holstered his six-shooter. Wrapping his arms around the boy, he rubbed his arms, trying to generate warmth. But, his own skin stung as if tiny razor blades sliced into him. It was the same feeling he got whenever he sensed trouble. "Son, you're freezin' to death. What the hell you doin' out here alone this time of night?"

The boy blinked teary eyes. He spoke through trembling lips. "Please. Save. Mary."

***

Jimmy Pierce studied the boy whose porcelain white face, almost like an unnatural mask, seemingly glowed against the orange flames of the campfire. Wisps of blond hair fell from underneath a two-sizes too big hat. So it wasn't his wide-brimmed hat. The large gray coat, a tent over his bony frame, also couldn't be his. What the hell? Who was this young one out in the wild on his own?

The boy refused food. Wouldn't drink water. Or even sit. His lips, nearly blue from the cold, quivered. His chin shook as if he would cry again.

Pierce frowned. He thought to voice his curiosity about the stranger but kept his mouth shut. The two Marshals would just tell him to shut up anyways. But something wasn't right.

And the boy's story was the stuff of nightmares.

Marshal Tuck wrapped a blanket around the boy's shoulder. Snowflakes quickly gathered on the heavy brown cloth. "Jacob, your mind ain't right. You've been out in the cold. It's taken its toll. Made you crazy."

The boy named Jacob shook his head. Fresh tears formed. "No, I speak truth. My sister Mary... they going to kill her at dawn. If thou won't help me, send me on away. I'll find someone who will. Have to save Mary."

RESURRECTION

Marshal Whitman hugged his Winchester. "Who's goin' to kill her?"

Jacob's thin legs failed him. He dropped into the dirt. He wiped his reddened eyes. Raised his voice. "The town elders! They thinking God demands a sacrifice. That's why the river won't bring no more gold. If they sacrifice Mary, God will bring back the gold. They say it's in the Bible. Mister, I got gold coins if thou help. More back home, too." The boy reached into his trouser pocket and with a shaky hand lifted a pouch. "Look. Real gold. Take it. Just help me save Mary."

Pierce lifted his chin. *Gold?* His pulse quickened. Thoughts swirled. To hell with his suspicions. Maybe if they helped this little mouse, Pierce could find a way to escape, take the gold and help his own family. It was a worth a try. "Marshal, I think we should—"

"I don't want to hear from you, Jimmy." Marshal Tuck scratched his chin. This couldn't be true. This young one was just in shock. "Jacob, where is this town you speak of? Where's your home? Your ma and pa?"

Jacob pointed to the mountains. "There, a mining town in them hills. Called Resurrection. My pa died two winters ago in the mines. Ma belongs to Reverend Jeremiah now. Mary takes care of me. Good care of me. I stole this horse. The clothes. Rode out to find help. Please, Mister. Please."

Marshal Tuck chewed on his upper lip. Who the hell would name a town Resurrection? Then again who would name their town Tombstone, like those firewater drunks in Arizona. He leaned over, then patted the boy on the shoulder. "Son, you rest a spell. I need to talk to my partner."

The boy brushed away his hand. "But Mary!"

"Yes, I know. Let me ponder this a moment." Marshal Tuck signaled Bill Whitman to join him. They stepped away from the fire, their backs to the boy.

Marshal Whitman was the first to speak. Softly. Out of the side of his mouth. The hollow sensation in his gut told him to stay out of Resurrection. No good could come from a sidetrack from their main mission. Get Jimmy Pierce back to Arizona to hang. "What you gnawin' on, Sam? I know you. You want to help this boy, huh? You can't help yourself."

Marshal Tuck grinned. He kept his voice low. "We can't just leave the young one out here in the snow. He'll die. His story is plumb crazy. Don't believe it for a second. But, it can't hurt to get him home to his family?"

A coyote howled in the distance. Followed by a second. Marshal Whitman glanced toward the night sky at a moon fighting to break through the clouds. Its light drenched the clouds in a ghostly white glow.

"Sam, that snow ain't lettin' up. We could be stuck there if a storm kicks up. You really want to be trapped in a town called Resurrection?" Marshal Whitman squeezed his shoulder blades together. He tried to ignore the chill crawling up his back. "I don't like it, Sam. Don't like it at all."

His older partner nudged him in the arm. "Bill, you gettin' scared on me? I know you ain't one for the Bible, but—"

"But nothin'." Marshal Whitman shifted his boots in the shallow layer of snow dusting the ground. "Sam, let's skip this one."

Sam Tuck shook his head. His partner was right, of course. This boy brought nothin' but trouble. Trouble they didn't need. But, they carried a badge, and that meant somethin'. "Sorry, Bill. What kind of lawmen would we be if we left this boy to fend for himself? No, we get him home, then be on our way. I promise. There ain't goin' to be a storm. This snow will let up by morn. We hand this young one over to his ma, then we get Jimmy to the territorial prison."

With a heavy sigh, Bill lamented. "If you say so, Sam. But if this boy be the death of me, I'll come back from the grave and bury my boot so far up your rear, you'll never get it out. You hear me?"

Marshal Tuck chuckled. "Quit your bellyachin'."

He turned back to Jacob, who had silently crossed to them and stood straight as a statue an arm's length away. His doll face rigid. Eyes unblinking. Head tilted to one side. His fingers interlocked just under his chin.

Marshal Tuck's hand instinctively gripped the handle of his .45, but he kept it holstered. He lowered to one knee, glaring at Jacob, "Gal-dang, boy. Give a warnin' next time you approach a man with a gun, else you might find yourself with a bullet in your belly."

Jacob tilted his head to the other side. "Will thou help me save Mary?"

Marshal Tuck nodded. "Can you lead us back to Resurrection in the dark?"

"Yes, sir." Jacob bounced up and down on his feet.

"Then, let's be on our way." Marshal Tuck lifted himself to his feet. He turned to the horses. "Let's break—"

Jacob threw his arms around Marshal Tuck's legs. "I thank thou." He separated from the Marshal, then lifted the pouch of gold coins. "Here, take it."

"Keep it." I ain't lookin' for payment. "Let's just get you home. Make sure you and your sister are safe."

Marshals Tuck and Whitman busied themselves, saddling the horses. Pierce, still chained to the oak, watched them. *Good. I reckon just one mistake on their part and I'll be makin' my escape. And maybe get some of that gold.*

The boy walked by the tree, stopping in front of him. Pierce nodded. *Let's all be friendly like.* "Don't worry none, boy. Them Marshals are good men. They'll save your sister."

A wide, twisted grin crossed the boy's face from ear to ear. His eyes bulged. His tongue slowly slid across his teeth. Then, the smile drifted away. His face shifted to stone. He stared blankly at Pierce for another heartbeat before continuing toward his horse.

What the hell was that? Pierce's saliva stuck in his throat. The hair on his neck stiffened. He swallowed his phlegm and released a lungful of hot air. The mist from his breath hovered around his face. His body shivered but not from the cold.

***

They rode through the frozen night into the hills past ancient oaks and willows, the limbs creaking like Marshal Tuck's old bones. To their good fortune, the snow had long since let up, but the moon had never again shown itself—its glow forever hidden behind thick, dark clouds. But as the morning hours approached, their luck did not hold true. A mist settled over the land, boxing in their view to a few feet in any direction.

Marshal Whitman cursed under his breath. How long until daybreak? If only that first light would show itself. *Damn fool thing we be doin'!*

Marshal Tuck kept his eyes on the boy riding just ahead of him. "Jacob, are we close?"

"Not far." The boy responded without looking back.

Pierce rode beside Marshal Tuck. Had to. The Marshal tied a rope between their saddles. And Pierce's hands remained shackled. An uncomfortable way to ride, but he managed. He, too, kept his eyes on the boy, but from time to time he gazed at the rifle nestled tightly against the side of Marshal Tuck's horse. If he had his chance, he'd grab that weapon, but who to kill? The lawmen? Or that boy?

Jacob pulled back on the reins. His horse slid to a stop between two towering trees whose branches touched, like gnarled fingers crisscrossing. The others slowed. They stopped just behind him.

The boy blinked his large eyes. He pointed beyond the trees. "There. Against the hillside. That's Resurrection."

Marshal Tuck rubbed his chin with a gloved hand. He gazed through the heavy mist at a town seemingly built into a mountain, layer upon layer with the narrowest of trails—just wide enough for one wagon at a time to pass—climbing through the town. And it was quiet. Too quiet. Except for the gurgling of a stream he couldn't yet see. How could a town be so silent with daybreak so near? *Strange!*

He reached into a saddlebag tied to the side of his horse and grabbed a brass spyglass, scratched and scuffed with time. Placing it to one eye, he scanned for signs of morning activity. Nothing. *Damn strange.*

The mist hid much of the town. A few wooden structures were visible. A church with a cross atop a steeple was just off the path a short ride up the hillside. Farther up, black smoke climbed from what could have been cabins. Darkened windows hid anyone inside. Anyone who might be watching them. Marshal Tuck clenched his teeth. He continued his search. Even higher up, rising above everything else, was a mill with a paddlewheel, which meant there must be water high up the hillside. A light flickered in one of the mill's window, but it vanished. Or had he imagined it? His thoughts raced. Heart pounded. They'd done their job. Brought the boy back home. They should ride away. But curiosity tingled his insides. Was there really a Mary? Could she be in danger?

He handed the spyglass to Marshal Whitman, then urged his horse to join Jacob's. "Why don't I see anyone up this morning?"

Jacob's eyes flitted nervously from the town to Marshal Tuck. "Reverend Jeremiah is very strict. None can be outside until the Lord's light shines."

Marshal Whitman stared through the spyglass. The hairs on the back of his neck were on high alert. "Why?"

Jacob lifted his oversized hat from his eyes. "Reverend Jeremiah says people will do evil in the dark."

Pierce pursed his lips. He sniffed the air. A stench, like rotten food, drifted from the hillside. "What the hell does that mean?"

Jacob shrugged. "I don't know, Mister. All I know is they going to kill Mary when the sun's first light touches Rival. We don't have much time." He pointed his thin forefinger at the mill. "Just beyond there. That's where the mines are. That's where they keeping her. Please, they going to kill her unless we hurry."

Marshal Whitman leaned closer to Sam. He grimaced at his longtime partner. "Not likin' this, partner. You smell the air? Foul. No, don't like this one bit. But I guess you means to see it through. But promise me this, old man. If this turns into a gunfight, we get our hides out of here."

Marshal Tuck nodded. In a voice barely above a whisper, he said, "If this becomes a gunfight, that means this here boy wasn't crazy after all, and we'll have to save his sister. We're lawmen, Bill. Remember that."

Pierce was close enough to hear. He wrestled against the shackles, cringing as the steel cut into his skin. "I ain't no lawman, though. What say you leave me out of this. I'll be waitin' here for you. How about that?"

Marshal Tuck shook his head. "Sorry, Pierce. We ride together."

"Well, how about you see yourself to hand me one of your guns, Marshal?" Pierce pointed a finger at Marshal Tuck's six-shooter.

"Sorry again." Marshal Tuck nudged his horse forward. The steed hesitated. Its neck muscles quivered. Head shook. Finally, the beast yielded to Marshal's Tuck's command. "Let's go, boys. See what Resurrection has to offer. Lead on, Jacob."

"Yes, sir." Jacob turned back to Marshal Tuck, a wide grin on his face. "I thank thee for believing me." The grin vanished as quickly as it formed. Young Jacob gazed forward, eyes unblinking. He led his horse past the trees to the dirt path into Resurrection.

The three men followed. The heavy mist parted for them as if a doorway opening but closed again behind them.

Marshal Whitman peered over his shoulder. The trail behind them was now hidden by a wall of gray fog. Releasing his horse's reins, he checked to make sure his Winchester was loaded. When finished, he grasped the chipped, scratched handle of his holstered revolver and lifted the tarnished gun to his face. The old Colt was fully loaded. But his unease hung over him like a weight bearing down on his shoulders.

Marshal Tuck stopped his horse at the outskirts of town. A sign on a wooden post had Resurrection etched into it. Along with the message, *Let he who enters bow down to the Almighty, for the blood of non-believers shall be spilt, so sayeth the Lord.* He fingered the handle of his .45. "Must be friendly folk," he uttered.

Pierce wrinkled his nose. Try as he might, he couldn't block the stink of whatever rot spread through Resurrection. He also couldn't keep his body from shivering. Ice filled his insides. A cold sweat formed across his brow. *Ignore it. Stick to your plan. Wait for your chance, then make your escape. Find your way home to your daughter. You can still make good on your promise to give her a good life.*

RESURRECTION

The trail through Resurrection led up the hillside, past log cabins seemingly built into the jagged rocks. If people lived inside, no one came out to greet them. Darkened windows did little to reveal who might be watching them. The town remained bathed in silence, except for the gurgling stream and the thud of their horses' hooves, until...

A creak sounded behind them. Marshal Tuck swung around in his saddle, Colt in hand. Nothing. They were still alone. He gazed at his partner. Marshal Whitman aimed his Winchester in the direction of the sound. They exchanged a long look but said nothing. Then continued on their way, climbing higher into Resurrection.

They passed the church, not much more than an aging wooden barn, titling to one side. A series of uneven steps led to thick double doors. A window to the left of the door was cracked. Something black stained the wood just beneath the window. Marshal Tuck recognized such a stain. He'd been a lawman long enough to identify the remnants of dried blood. But what town didn't have blood stains?

The path through town wound upward, passing a mercantile. Pierce glanced at the sign above the front door. *God's Glory Hardware. Serving Only True Believers.* A wagon missing a wheel and tipped to one side was outside the store. Though empty, a swarm of flies circled just above the wagon. A rocking chair sat beneath a window. Was it rocking on its own? Pierce glared at it. No, it must be his imagination.

Jacob led them from one log cabin to the next but still no people. No horses. No dog wandering aimlessly in the darkness. No signs of life. As if Resurrection had been abandoned. Marshal Tuck rubbed his nose. The stench was getting worse the farther up the path they traveled. And the flies from the wagon seemed to follow them, buzzing the horses' heads, latching to their eyes as if to feast on the crusting tears that formed just below the steeds' eyelids.

They finally reached the mill high above the town. Marshal Whitman lifted his hat and raked his fingers through his sweaty hair. From this high point, much of the town they'd passed lay hidden under layers of gray mist. Only the church steeple and its large cross were clearly visible, cutting through the fog like a blade ripping through flesh. He shuddered. But why? How many towns had he passed through? More than he could remember. So why was Resurrection making his hands clammy? His skin itch?

He turned to the mill. Built from stone, it stood two stories with a roof that had partially caved in. A wooden paddlewheel on the right side moaned in protest, forced to turn by a narrow stream that passed by. The flowing water seemingly disappeared into the rocky hillside. The only way to reach the mill was by crossing a plank bridge just a few feet above the water. Whitman guided his horse up to the bridge. It was missing a plank or two. Why would the townsfolk let Resurrection fall into such a festering waste?

His gaze shifted from the bridge to the stream. He thought for a moment about filling his extra canteen, but the water was black, murky. More flies skimmed the surface. Not what a fresh mountain spring should look like, even under the cover of night.

Jacob rode his horse further upstream. He turned again to Marshal Tuck. His eyes bulged. Cheeks quivered. Deep lines formed across his forehead. His eyebrows nearly touched. "Sir, just up ahead is the mine where Mary be. We have to hurry. Before dawn. If Reverend Jeremiah finds us, he'll punish me. Hurt thee."

Marshal Tuck tightened his grip on his six-shooter. "Jacob, this town of yours seems abandoned."

The boy furiously shook his head. "No, they only sleep. The Reverend Jeremiah. The other elders. They are very scary. They'll kill her. They believe it the only way to bring back the gold."

Pierce rolled his eyes. Snorted. When would he be able to make his move?

Marshal Whitman rode up to Jacob. "Listen, boy, if you speak the truth, we should get the upper hand on 'em while they sleep. Surprise 'em in their cabins. I'll kill that reverend myself if I have to."

Jacob tilted his head to the side. A tear slid down one cheek. "Thou cannot kill the reverend."

"Enough." Marshal Tuck lifted his second revolver from his saddlebag. "I've had just about—"

A scream broke the early morning quiet. A girl's scream. From up ahead. Where Jacob had pointed to the mine.

"My Mary!" Jacob flicked his horse's reins. The steed charged over the bridge, beyond the mill, farther up the hillside.

"Damnit." Marshal Tuck exchanged a long glance with his partner, then called out, "Yah!" His steed chased after the boy.

Pierce's horse, still attached by a rope, was forced to follow.

Marshal Whitman closed his eyes and under his breath mumbled a quick prayer. Squeezing the reins, clenching his teeth, he leaned in close to his horse's ear. "Let's go, Betsy, but keep your eyes open."

The mine was less than a stone's throw up the hillside. Jacob was the first to reach the entrance, but Marshal Tuck and Pierce were close behind. Pierce wished he could pinch his nose. The stench was worse here. And the flies. So many of them. Swarming around the opening. Their buzz almost deafening. As if a warning to stay out. A warning he would rather heed. But if entering was the one way to gain his freedom, he'd do it. What choice did he have? Take a chance on overpowering the lawmen in the darkness of a mineshaft or die on a hangman's noose back in Yuma.

Jacob climbed from his horse and started toward the entrance, "We have to hurry, Marshal!"

Marshal Tuck slid from his horse, armed now with two six-shooters. "Slow yourself, boy." He studied the entrance. A horseshoe-shaped hole cut int the hillside buttressed with cracking timber. Just large enough for a man to enter. An icy darkness beyond the opening was like an impenetrable wall hiding whatever lay beyond his vision. And what the hell was that wretched odor? It was enough to make a man sick. But, like he told his partner, they were lawmen. They didn't turn away when someone needed help. And right now…

Another scream spilled from the mine. Followed by a girl's terrified plea. "Please, no! Leave me be!"

Jacob dashed inside. "Mar—"

Marshal Whitman grabbed him by his oversized jacket, yanking him back. He placed a gloved hand over the boy's mouth. With a finger to his own lips, the Marshal whispered, "Shhhh."

The girl cried out again. "Please, don't hurt me!"

Marshal Tuck holstered his six-shooters. Bending to the ground, he lifted a broken tree branch. He then retrieved a dirty cloth from his saddlebag and a match. He wrapped the cloth around one end of the branch and struck the match across his course jacket. When ignited, he lit the cloth, turning it into a crackling, orange flamed torch. "Follow me."

Pierce, now off his horse, shook his head. "If I be goin' in there, shouldn't you take these damn shackles off?"

Marshal Tuck scowled at Jimmy. "No, but thanks for remindin' me you'll be joinin' us. You take the lead. I'll keep the barrel of this here gun buried in the small of your back just in case you have any ideas." He looked down at Jacob. "Boy, stay here where it's safe."

Jacob grabbed Marshal Tuck's arm. "No, sir. Have to save Mary. I'm coming with thee."

Marshal Tuck sighed. The boy had courage. Maybe he was safer stickin' with them. "Fine but stay behind me."

Pointing the burning torch toward the mine, he motioned to Pierce. "Lead the way, Jimmy. And don't think about tryin' anything, else I'll fill you with so much led, your final breath will be in this rotten, stinkin' hole."

Pierce glowered at him. "You're all heart, Marshal."

Scrunching his nose, Pierce crept into the mineshaft. Flies quickly gathered around his head, brushing against his cheek. He ducked to avoid them, but it did little good. "Blasted. Blood sucking bastards."

He inched deeper inside. Ahead of him, nothing but a bleak passage large enough maybe for two men to work side by side swinging hammers. But it was hard to tell the full size. Thick blackness shrouded his view.

Marshal Tuck, right behind him, jabbed the torch into the darkness just over Pierce's shoulder. The dancing flames dimmed as if the mine tried to smother the light. But the orange glow was enough to reveal a jagged, curved passage. Roughly cut stone littered the pathway. Buy there was something else. He aimed the torch toward the ground.

His body stiffened. His heart raced. He bent on one knee to make sure his eyes weren't deceiving him in the shadows of the mine.

A human skull rested on its side among the rocks.

Pierce backed away. His mouth fell agape. "What am I seein?"

Marshal Whitman, his Winchester held close to his side, lowered to his partner. His stomach churned.

He tried to spit, but his dry mouth couldn't produce the saliva. "Sam, this ain't right."

"What is it, Marshal?" Jacob asked.

"Don't look, boy." Marshal Tuck stood and pushed ahead a few steps deeper into the shaft. He waved the torch out in front of him. More skulls lined the passage. Other dismembered bones—arms, feet, legs—were strewn about. Skeletal hands, some with bits of flesh, protruded from the walls.

Hot bile rose up Marshal Whitman's throat. He forced it back down. "Is this some kind of burial chamber?" The stench of rotting flesh filled his nose, coating his membranes. He couldn't shake it. And the buzzing flies rattled his brain. "Sam, let's get the hell out of here. This ain't no place—"

"Marshal?" Jacob started toward him.

"I said stay…"

Another scream, this time close, echoed through the shaft.

"Mary!" Jacob bolted away from them. He stumbled into the darkness, scrambling over the bones, as if ignoring them all together.

"Damn, kid." Marshal Tuck followed, leaving Pierce's side.

Pierce turned back toward the mine entrance. This was the chance he was waiting for. A chance to escape. Find his way back to his daughter.

RESURRECTION

The cold barrel of Marshal Whitman's Winchester stopped him. "You ain't goin' nowhere, Jimmy."

Pierce stomped his foot. "Come on, Marshal. You said it yourself. This ain't right. Let's get out of this hole."

Bill Whitman raised the barrel to Jimmy's face. Sure, he wanted out of this hellhole, but he would never abandon Sam Tuck. Never. "We ain't leavin' my partner behind. Now get movin.'"

Pierce lowered his head. *Damn, stupid lawmen. We're all goin' to die here. We're already in our graves. Don't they get it?*

With Marshal Whitman's rifle pressing against his back, Pierce continued through the shaft, following the trail of light bouncing off the walls from Marshal Tuck's torch. Their own heavy breaths were as loud as the buzzing flies. Pierce's pulse beat so loudly it was like a drum in his ears. His chest ached.

They rounded a corner. Found the lit torch laying on the ground. A pair of gloved hands grabbed hold of Pierce's arm and tugged him to his knees. It was Marshal Tuck. He and the boy knelt behind a large stone. The Marshal mouthed the word, *quiet.* Then motioned with his eyes to peer ahead. A bead of sweat dripped down the side of his face despite the mine's stinging chill.

Pierce pressed his back against the shaft's wall. He gazed into a large chamber ablaze in an orange flush from a single torch held by a large figure in a dark cloak. A second stranger, draped in a similar cloak but shorter, stood beside the first. The fire cast their formless bodies as massive shadows sprawling against the chamber's walls. Pierce inched forward, his back sliding against the damp stone. He rubbed his fingers together. Breathed as silently as possible. Beyond the cloaked figures was a cell with someone trapped behind the bars. *Jesus, was the boy right? Had he been telling the truth?*

One of the figures lifted an object from his cloak. A key. With a deep male voice, the stranger spoke. "Child, thy time has come to sacrifice thy life for the greater good." He jammed the key into a lock. Turned it until a click echoed through the chamber. The cell door creaked as he swung it open. "I hope thou will willing give thyself so that Resurrection can rise again."

"No, I don't want to die!" She backed away from the cloaked figures.

Jacob tried to launch himself from his hiding place, but Marshal Tuck wrapped his arms around the boy and shook his head. "Don't be a damn fool," he whispered. Then, to Marshal Whitman. "You ready?"

"I guess." Marshal Whitman raised his Winchester. His blood pumped fast through his veins. A tiny flame ignited in his chest, warming his body, his limbs. "Partner, I'll follow your lead."

Marshal Tuck pointed at Jacob. "Stay back."

The boy nodded.

The Marshal leaned closer to Pierce. "Jimmy, I be askin' for your help. You do this, and you might just earn yourself a pardon." Marshal Tuck took one of his .45s and handed it to Pierce. He then unlocked his shackles. "And the boy's gold is yours for the takin'."

Marshal Whitman started to protest but held his tongue.

Pierce gripped the warm handle of the revolver. Finally. It felt good in his hands. This was his chance. Kill them. Run out of there. And keep runnin' till he found his way home. To his wife. His daughter. His lovely daughter with a gentle smile and good soul. Damn, she'd want him to stay and help this little girl. How could he ever face her knowing he'd been a coward? He'd run when another child needed him. He locked eyes with Marshal Tuck. Besides, a pardon and some gold sounded good. He made up his mind. "Let's save this little one and get the hell out of here."

They slinked into the chamber, tiptoeing to the cell, Marshal Tuck in the lead but his partner and Pierce beside him. Marshal Tuck flipped his revolver around so that he gripped the barrel. He willed his old bones not to creak. Kept his breathing silent. Despite his years, he was still good at the hunt. Quick to overcome his prey. He squeezed the barrel until his knuckles, hidden under his gloves, turned white. He raised the weapon over his head.

Reaching the closest cloaked figure, the shorter of the two, he mumbled just loud enough for them to hear, "Hey."

The shorter stranger swung around. But not fast enough to avoid the handle of Marshal Tuck's six-shooter crashing against his head. The thwack rippled through the chamber. Before the stranger could utter a yelp, the Marshal struck him a second and third time. The crack of a skull shattering into pieces pierced the Marshal's ears. Blood sprayed onto his revolver. Onto his face. The stranger, a bearded man, toppled to his side. He didn't move. Didn't groan. Blood leaked through his hood, dribbling onto the rocky ground.

The taller stranger whipped around. A single strike from the butt of Marshal Whitman's rifle smashed his cheek. His hood flew off. Bone tore through flesh. The man's head jolted to the side. His legs crumbled beneath him. He dropped to the ground, his body motionless. Blood pooled around his broken face.

RESURRECTION

From the cell, the young girl shrieked.

"Mary, don't be afraid!" Jacob ran to her. "These be good men. Come to save thee. I brought them here, Mary. I did good." He wrapped his arms around the girl he called Mary. His head just reached her chest.

Mary hugged him tight. "Jacob, I knew thou would save me."

Marshal Tuck approached them both. He now grasped his .45's bloody handle. The girl gazed up at him with crystal blue eyes, very different from Jacob's. But her porcelain white skin matched his. Long blond hair, fiery against the torch's dancing flame, fell wildly around her shoulders. She was a skinny thing. Almost bony. Her stiff gray dress, buttoned up to her neck, hung loosely from her wispy frame. Had they been starving her. "Are you okay? Can you walk?" the Marshal asked.

"I think so." Her voice trembled. "Are thou going to hurt me like the others?"

Marshal Tuck shook his head. He glared at the two fallen men. They still breathed. For now. What kind of animals were they?

Pierce cleared his throat. "Uh, I think we best be gettin' out of here before more of these freaks show up."

Another voice, deep and throaty, responded from behind them. "Brothers, that would not be very kind of thee."

Marshal Tuck whipped his Colt around, aiming the barrel in the direction of the voice. He faced a gathering of men and women, their bodies hidden in the shadows. Faces obscured by a gloom that not even the torch's flame could penetrate. They stood shoulder to shoulder. Like statues. Arms down at their sides. Heads slightly titled. In the bleakness, Marshal Tuck couldn't count their numbers. Maybe the whole town stood before them. And they blocked the only way out.

One stood taller than the rest. He struck a match and lighted a pipe. Puffing on it until smoke formed. An orange radiance encircled his face. Marshal Tuck aimed his .45 at the man's head. The barrel was straight. Unwavering. The man had a long, thin face covered by a graying beard down to his chest. Black circles surrounded his eyes. Deep lines, liked cracks in his porcelain skin, spread across his forehead. A patch of pale skin dangled loose from his cheek. As the pipe's glow slowly faded, the man straightened the collar of his long black coat and stepped away from the others, breaching the soft orange haze from the torch.

RESURRECTION

He took one more puff on the pipe, then slowly removed it from between his lips. A wide smile crossed his face. His eyes, large and gray, were unblinking. "Brothers, thou have no business here."

Jacob and Mary whimpered, clinging to Marshal Tuck's trousers.

Marshal Tuck didn't need to ask the name of the man. It was already clear to him, but he did anyway. "Would I be addressing, Reverend Jeremiah?"

"Why, yes brother." The reverend peered down at the two fallen men. He shook his head. "Why have thou harmed two of my flock?"

Marshal Tuck didn't answer that question. "I'm a federal lawman. Same as my partner there with the Winchester. We be takin' this here girl and her brother and leaving your town without any further trouble. Just back away and clear a path. No one else need be hurt, understand?"

The reverend chuckled, like a hyena's cackle, but quickly became gravely silent. His face turned grim. "Why, brothers, thou are in Resurrection. We don't recognize thy authority here. We follow God's word. That is our law. And only Godly men and women are allowed in our holy town."

Marshal Tuck inched forward. Muscles tensed. "That may be, but I'm still takin' these children. Then, I'll leave your town in peace."

Reverend Jeremiah lifted his pipe to his mouth and took a long drag. Smoke hovered around his face. "Thou are mistaken, brother. The girl belongs to us, and she has not yet fulfilled her life's purpose. We cannot permit her to go, especially with a non-believer."

"My Winchester would differ with you." Marshal Whitman stepped in front of his partner. Rage made his cheeks burn. "Friend, if you don't do as my partner says, I'll bury a bullet in your head. Trust me, I'm a good shot."

The reverend held out his hands, palms up. His fingers, long and gnarled, were more bone than flesh. The grin returned to his face. "I have no weapon, brother. The Lord is my shepherd. I shall not want. I have no need for thy crude creations. No, brother, if thou wishes to take my life, it shall be done, but thou will not remove the girl from us. Her purpose will soon be revealed as will thine."

Reverend Jeremiah turned to the townspeople people behind him. Extending his arms as if to embrace them all, he raised his voice and spoke like a loving father. "My flock, show them the way."

The townspeople did as their reverend directed. Stepping from the shadows, they lumbered toward Marshal Whitman, Marshal Tuck, Jimmy Pierce and the two children, uttering, "Show them the way," over and over. Their eyes never blinked. Their expressions remained stonelike. Their bodies stiff.

The children cried out.

Marshal Whitman cursed.

Marshal Tuck pulled the trigger of his .45. The thunderous crack exploded through the chamber. The screaming lead instantly found its target. The back of Reverend Jeremiah's head. Bone and brain matter flew in every direction. Blood splashed across the townspeople. The reverend's head snapped forward. He dropped to his knees. A final breath exhaled from his lips, and he collapsed to the ground. Blood spilled from a large hole in the back of his skull, coating the chamber's rocky floor. Dripping onto the boots of those closest to the body.

The townspeople stopped... for a heartbeat. In unison, they peered down at their fallen leader. Then, one by one, they glared at the three men standing before them and the two children. Their chanting soon returned. "Show them the way." With heavy steps, they plodded forward, stepping over the reverend, smearing their boots with his blood.

Marshal Tuck, his heart pounding, turned to Pierce. Bill and I... we'll clear a path! You take the children! Don't look back! No matter what!"

Pierce nodded.

Without further words, the two marshals stepped forward, opening fire, their weapons erupting with fury. Round after round struck the townspeople. They screamed, their bodies crumbling over each other. But more kept coming. With sure hands, Marshal Tuck reloaded. Fired again. But they wouldn't stop. Their chanting continued. "Show them the way."

"Go!" Marshal Tuck shouted.

Pierce's mind jumbled. The Marshal's words were like a distant call he could barely hear over the ringing in his ears from the burst of hot lead. What was happening? Was this a nightmare? It couldn't be real. But it was. Damnit, it was! Shaking his head, he turned to the children. "Hold onto my belt! Don't let go! No matter what!"

Marshal Tuck and Marshal Whitman threw themselves into the townspeople, firing their last rounds. When their bullets were spent, they swung wildly with the butt of their weapons.

Pierce charged ahead, the children in tow. Stumbling over fallen bodies, he scrambled through the chamber toward the mineshaft. A man grabbed his shoulder. Pierce fired a round pointblank into the man's face. His flesh nearly disintegrated into bone fragments and a haze of blood. A woman grabbed the girl by the hair. Pierce turned his revolver on her. A round struck the woman in the chest. She fell backward, her body piling onto others.

Without looking back, Pierce ran from the chamber into the shaft. One more man stood in his way. Pierce fired a third round. The bullet found the man's neck. He clutched his throat, coughing blood and gurgling, slumping to his knees. Kicking the man in the head, Pierce grabbed onto the children and pulled them through the shaft.

Up ahead was the opening.

Morning light cut through the darkness. His pulse racing, chest heaving, he aimed his six-shooter dead ahead. He had a couple of bullets left. If anyone blocked their path, they'd die like the others.

Without breaking stride, he passed through the entrance into the light of a gray winter morning. Snow had started to fall again, blanketing the town in a white cover. But there were no townspeople waiting for them. *Thank God!* And their horses were still there… untouched. How could that be?

Peering back into the mineshaft, he saw only darkness. No one followed. No sign of either Marshal. No more crack of their weapons.

Jacob and Mary stood beside them, each crying hysterically. Jacob embraced his sister. She kept looking back into the shaft.

Pierce placed a hand on their shoulders. "I need you two to trust me. We're goin' to jump on that there horse." He pointed to the ginger steed. "And we're goin' to ride out of here. And we won't stop until we find the next town. And a sheriff."

Hoisting Jacob onto the horse, Pierce climbed up behind him, then extended a hand to Mary. She eagerly grabbed on and swung onto the horse behind him. Pierce slapped the side of the beast and called out, "Yah."

The steed galloped away, rushing by the mill. Over the bridge. Through the town. Down the hillside. Still no townspeople in the way. Resurrection was as quiet as when they had ridden in under the cover of early morning darkness.

They cleared the town, racing into the Colorado wild. Snow whipped Pierce in the face. He ignored it, peering over his shoulder. Still no one followed. His heart beat even faster. They'd made it out alive. Somehow. They were free. Safe.

"We a goin' to make..."

Something jabbed into Pierce's lower back. The point ripped deeper and deeper into his flesh, slowly cutting through muscle and nerves. A grating cry rose from his throat. Then, whatever it was tore free, slicing more skin as it was ripped from his back. Agonizing pain radiated throughout his body. He twisted around. The girl... Mary... held a blood-soaked blade in her hand. Her head titled, she smiled at him. With crazed eyes opened wide, she chanted, "Show him the way."

"Why...." With his steed still in full gallop, Pierce slid from the beast, crashing onto the ground with a thud that stole his breath. "Uhhh!" He rolled several times, his arms and legs thrashing about wildly, the world around him spinning. He came to a stop on his back, his legs twisted unnaturally. He gasped, struggling for air that just wouldn't move in and out of his burning lungs. Darkness closed in. A numbness settled over his body.

He tried to rise onto his elbows, but the movement sparked white-hot pain in his back. He cried out. Reaching toward his back, his hand found his injury. Blood spilled over his fingers. He gazed at his blood-drenched fingers with dimming eyes. He coughed, trying to force a little air through his throat.

Jacob and Mary casually approached him, each with a brimming smile. Pierce tried to slide away, but his body wouldn't heed his command.

Mary leaned down to him. A blush appeared across her porcelain skin. She still didn't blink her crystal blue eyes. She seemed to study him, then her eyes drifted to the blade in her hands. She gazed at the blood dripping off the tip. Let a drop fall onto her finger and licked it with her tongue. A giggle escaped her lips. "The reverend will be so proud of us."

Jacob's grin disappeared. Like he'd done before, he slid his tongue over his teeth. A sneer parted his lips.

"Why... are you... doin'... this?" Pierce's voice limped from his throat. His heart slowed. Chest barely moved up and down. This... had... to be... a nightmare. He... would... wake up... and be safe.

"All will be revealed soon." Jacob lifted his boot and smashed it into the side of Pierce's head.

Pierce felt the skull-rattling blow.

But nothing else.

Darkness overcame him.

***

The pain returned. His head pounded. His back spasmed with jolting pain as if he'd been stabbed all over again. His mind spun out of control. The mineshaft. The chamber. The reverend. The townspeople. The blade digging into his flesh. It all came rushing back. Consciousness returned. His eye flittered open. At first, his surroundings were hazy. He blinked over and over. Light replaced the dark.

But the pain was like a hot iron burning into his flesh.

"What… the… hell." Pierce's words were little more than a mumble.

Another voice filled his ears. The reverend's. "Good, brother. Thou have returned to us. Now open thy eyes and behold thy true purpose in life."

How could the reverend be speakin'? He was killed in the mine, wasn't he? His head exploded into a horrific mess of shattered bone, pieces of brain and a puddle of blood. Pierce blinked again. His vision slowly cleared. His lower lip dropped. Reverend Jeremiah stood before him as if he'd never been shot. As if he hadn't died a gruesome, violent death.

"You… died."

The reverend shook his head. The flap of skin along his cheek dipped farther down his face. "No, brother, thy weapons cannot kill those of Resurrection. The Lord is our shield."

Behind him, the woman and the two men Pierce killed stood in silence. And all the others gunned down inside the mine were beside them. They held hands, grins across their pale faces. All resurrected from the dead. No signs of the mortal wounds they suffered. Not even a drop of blood on their drab clothing. How could this be? Nothing made sense.

Pierce focused again on the reverend. His hands were smothered in blood. But not his own. He held something in each palm. Pierce blinked again. *Oh my*

God! It can't be! In each hand the reverend grasped a pulsating heart. With each beat, more blood slid over the reverend's fingers.

His arms were outstretched and shackled to a piece of timber. His legs were also tethered to a piece of wood. His feet suspended just above the ground. He fought against his restraints, but it did no good. The effort robbed him of air. He coughed. Gasped. His lungs ached as if a heavy weight pressed against his chest, making it impossible to breathe. Fear tore through his body, like a crashing wave. *My God, these crazy bastards crucified me!*

He peered over his shoulder. Behind him was Resurrection's church. In front of him, the townspeople gathered behind the reverend, their eyes huge, bodies trembling. Some drooling. Snow blew across their faces, but they didn't budge. Their eyes locked on the hearts in the reverend's hands.

Pierce turned his head to the right. Marshal Tuck's body, his shirt removed revealing his chest, hung limply from another wooden cross. His head slumped against his neck. The flesh was torn away from his chest. His bones exposed. Blood spilled from the wound, dripping down his trousers onto the white snow. Pierce shook his head. He couldn't hold back a moan. A tremor ran through his limbs. His heartbeat thrashed in his ears.

Turning his head from Marshal Tuck, Pierce found Marshal Whitman also hung to a cross, his naked chest ripped open.

Pierce's heart sank deep within his chest. His jaw clenched. He lowered his eyes. Banged his head against the cross. Then, painfully lifting his chin, he spit at the reverend. "What have… you done… you sack of horseshit?"

Reverend Jeremiah smiled wide. "Brother, do not be angry and release thy fear, for today is a time to rejoice. That is why I wanted thee to awaken. Experience the joy of thy sacrifice just as thy friends did. And just as their lives will now serve a greater purpose, so shall thine."

"What… are… you… goin' on about?" Pierce kicked the cross with the back of his boot. Anything to break the timber. "We… came… to save… the girl. You… would kill her… to bring… back… the gold. Jacob… told… us."

The reverend peered over his shoulder. "Children, join us, please."

Mary and Jacob walked from behind the crowd and crossed to Reverend Jeremiah. They stopped at his side and lowered to their knees. Lifting their heads, they entwined their fingers under their chins as if in prayer. Smiles shredded their faces as if their skin would rip away.

"Father, are thou pleased?" Mary titled her head. Her blue eyes never blinked. Her smile was fixed to her face.

"Yes, my child." The reverend gazed at her, like a loving father.

"Father, we are so hungry." Jacob grasped the reverend's trousers. "We have been so good. May we eat?"

Reverend Jeremiah nodded. He lowered the hearts to both children. "Oh, yes, my boy. The time has come to feed. Hold out thy hands. But remember, just one bite. Thou must share. We all must share in our bounty."

Mary and Jacob held out their hands. The reverend placed the bloody hearts in their palms. Each child opened their mouths wide and took a bite. They twisted their heads back and forth until they ripped off a piece. Blood covered their mouths. Their teeth. When they were done, they licked away the red mess and tiny bits of flesh, then passed the hearts to the others. One by one, the townspeople hungrily bit into a heart, like ravenous dogs.

Pierce closed his eyes. *No! God!* What was he witnessing? His stomach turned over in revulsion.

"I am thankful, father," Mary uttered.

"Thou are welcome, child." The reverend patted her on the head. Blood dripped into her hair. She didn't seem to care.

Pierce's body trembled. "What…?" He struggled for a breath.

Reverend Jeremiah ignored him. He still gazed at Mary. "Child, fetch me my knife."

Pierce forced himself to speak. "I… don't… understand."

The reverend turned to Pierce and crossed to him, stopping just inches away. "Brother, first, forgive my little ruse to get thee here. I would never harm a member of my flock. We just needed a way to get thee to join us in Resurrection."

Pierce fought to keep his head from drooping. "Let… me… go."

"Brother, I cannot. But rejoice in knowing thy sacrifice will help to sustain my flock." The reverend ran his bloody fingers through his gray beard. "Let my words bring thee peace in thy final hour."

Pierce's eyes burned. He cried out, "Someone, help me!"

The Reverend placed a hand over Pierce's mouth. "Hear my words, brother. In the year of our Lord 1610, I led my people from Jamestown across this great land to practice our own way of observing the Lord. After much hardship, the Lord led us here, to Resurrection.

But there was no food. We were starving. So, some of our flock willingly sacrificed their bodies, so the rest could survive."

Mary ran up to the reverend. She handed him a long, thin knife, the blade already stained with blood.

"That is my sweet child." The reverend gripped the handle. "Now run along and play with thy brother."

She bowed, smiled at Pierce and skipped away.

Reverend Jeremiah studied the blade and circled Pierce. He continued the tale. Pierce unleashed a primal scream in the silence of his mind, but he couldn't drown out the reverend's words. "Brother, God help us, but we developed a taste for human flesh, and the Natives in this land became our prey. Then, something divine befell us. By chance. Be it the Lord's will. Of all the organs and parts of the flesh we fed upon, the human heart gave us new life. We never became sick. Never felt pain. Never grew any older. It was the Lord's gift. For over 200 years, he has sustained us as long as we feed. Not on each new day. Just when our old bodies start to stiffen. A few cracks appear in our skin." The reverend tore away the flap of skin from his cheek. "That's when the hunger sets in. That is when we hunt."

RESURRECTION

Pierce gritted his teeth. A wheezy, mucus-filled breath escaped his lips. "Why... not... kill... me... right away?"

Reverend Jeremiah stopped in front of Pierce, close enough to feel the reverend's hot breath brush against his cheek. "Yes, forgive me for that. Call it a personal liking, brother. I find the heart that has experienced exhilaration is the tastiest. When thou looked upon the wilds upon escaping us, I can only imagine the joy thee felt, brother." The reverend licked his lips. "Thy heart will be delicious."

The blade trembled in Reverend Jeremiah's hand. He raised the knife over his head. "I thank thee, brother."

Pierce shook his head. Begged for mercy. When none was offered, he cried out one last time. His final thought was of his daughter. His last vision - Jacob peeking through the crowd of townspeople. Smiling. Licking his teeth.

Then. Forever. Darkness.

Switched

Janet Post

I think I'm dying. I can't breathe and when I cough terrible pain shoots through my chest. I'm lying flat on my bed with my head propped up on a soft pillow. It's at a bad angle but I'm too weak to ask Abby to change it. My right arm is also propped on a pillow and a thin bandage encases my wrist. They must have bled me while I was asleep. Stupid practice, but doctors believe it helps.

"I see you're awake, Miss," Abby says in a strange voice. Abby has been my maid since I was a small girl. We are close in age and I know she loves me. I open my eyes and squint to see her. Everything is so cloudy and it's hard to focus.

I struggle to change my position and begin coughing. Abby rushes to my head and lifts me so it's easier to cough. She puts a handkerchief to my lips and tries to hide the red stain when she wipes my mouth. I truly am dying.

Why did I agree to meet Lion at night in the park? I knew it was going to rain. May in London can still be chilly. It had been cloudy all day. But I love Lionel even though my parents will never allow us to marry. His father is only a baronet with a small holding and Lion a second son. I allowed him one kiss and then it started raining. As I wore only a thin muslin dress and a light cloak, soon I was soaked to the skin. I was overcome with a coughing fit by the time I got back into the house. The next day I developed a raging fever and my mother called the doctor.

The doctor said I had influenza and prescribed a saline drought. When he left, Mother scolded me. She knew where I'd been. Her scolding took on a shrill tone as she berated me for dishonoring myself and my family, how she only wished me to have all the necessities of life and to be happy. Her voice sounded strangely stressed. I didn't care. Mother does not understand how much I love him. They think I will soon forget him after I've had a season in London. My mother assures me as beautiful as I am, and dressed in the finest new wardrobe, I will surely have many offers for my hand from men more acceptable to Father than Lion will ever be. Mother says I will go to balls, and Almacks, and many parties and meet men who are not a mere second son. They believe my love for Lion to be calf love and something I will soon recover from, but they are wrong.

After another horrid coughing fit, I realize I am surely dying. Mother will be sorry I suppose, though it is partly her fault. If she'd allowed me to see Lionel in my own home, I wouldn't have caught this wretched disease.

When I wake, Mother is standing over my bed staring at me with a strange cold expression on her face. When she sees I am awake, it changes to a warmer one, but I can still see the steel behind her icy-blue eyes. A woman is with her, an old crone with withered cheeks and strange eyes like black marbles staring at me from under heavy graying eyebrows. She holds a silver bowl in her hands with etched runes running across its sides.

"She's dying," Mother says to the crone.

"Yers, Miss," the old woman says. "Her time be almost upon her."

"She must live. We are all to pieces. George has gambled away everything. If Lilianna doesn't marry the duke, all will be lost." George is my father and even I am aware of his gambling habits. But what duke is mother speaking of? As sick as I am, I'm still shocked by her statements. We are all to pieces? Doesn't that mean we have no money and many debts?

"Abby," Mother calls my maid to her. "You would do anything for your mistress, wouldn't you?"

"Yes, Lady Everleigh. You know I would."

The old crone shakes her head. I feel so strange. I can only take shallow breaths and have to fight the urge to constantly cough. I ache everywhere and my face is burning hot. My vision is blurry, and everything is hazy, but I see the crone moving into Mother's place at my bedside. She takes my hand and places it on the side of the bowl. When she begins chanting my vision fades and my head spins.

"Are you sure this will work?" my mother asks the crone.

"As sure as I can be of anything," the crone says.

"You know I wouldn't ask you to do this if it wasn't my last resort, if I hadn't reached my wits end? Liliana is my only child. I can't lose her. All of our hopes are on her marrying well."

"Yes, my lady. I know you'd never have called on old Eliza if ye wasn't desperate. You done left your past behind along with the evil you done. As long as ye do yer part, old Eliza will do hers. You know what that is. You know what it is ye have to do."

Mother snarled. "Get me those diamonds and I'll keep my part of the bargain. Just do it."

"I be working on it. They ain't yers and shouldn't be, but ye done put me so's I have to do evil just like you. This could be permanent. Are ye sure ye want to do this?"

I heard their whispered conversation as though far away. I felt the cold silver of the strange bowl under my hands as Eliza resumed chanting. The bowl sang. I felt its song inside my soul. It drew me, it called to me, it pulled me out of my body. Before I knew it, I was whirling around and around inside the bowl. The sides were green agate shot through with gold threads. I whirled and spun. Not my body, but my essence, my spirit, was there in the bowl.

Eliza knelt beside Abby who lay unconscious on the floor of my bed chamber. How I knew this, I cannot tell. The old witch, for witch she must be, resumed chanting in a foreign language I didn't understand. The green sides of the bowl dimmed, and I floated out of the bowl to hover over Abby's prone body. The bowl sang to me again and I took a deep breath. It didn't hurt to breathe but I was so tired. I tried to open my eyes but failed and fell into a deep sleep.

Chapter Two

There was water under my head. My hair lay in the noxious liquid as well as the side of my face. I shivered with cold and my eyes were glued together. I rubbed them and took a deep breath. For the first time in weeks, it didn't hurt to breathe. I rolled onto my back and opened my eyes. Where was I? A light mist fell obscuring the hunched man climbing his step ladder to light the lamp on the corner of Halfmoon Street and Curzon. When he had it lit, I looked at my hand. My soft white hands were chapped and red, the nails neatly clipped, but my beautiful manicure was gone. This was not my hand.

Terror filled my heart. I patted my bodice and realized I was not wearing my nightdress. I touched my hair gingerly. It was loose, sopping wet, and when I lifted a lock, I saw it was red. I screamed and passed out cold.

I awoke for the second time to vigorous slaps being applied to my cheeks. "Miss, wake up. You can't lie here in the street. You'll get yerself runned over first thing some well-breeched swell drives his curricle down Curzon."

I groaned and allowed the lamplighter to lift me into a sitting position. I was wearing my maid's clothing. I had her half-boots of jean on my feet, her black skirt, white apron. The sleeves of her blouse, tied at the wrist, were filthy from the dirty water of the street. I was wearing Abby's clothing and had Abby's hands and hair; therefore, I must actually be Abby. How could this have happened?

The lamplighter left, carrying his ladder with him. The street was cold and dark outside the glow of the lamp. Where was my house? I crawled a few feet, then forced myself to stand. I was so dizzy and filled with fear I shook. I saw my house. Number 19. The house was dark save for one candle burning in my bedroom window, which faced the street. I pulled myself up the stairs and used the heavy knocker to bang on the door. It was flung open by Chadwick, our Second Footman. He looked down at me, placed his hand on my chest and pushed me off the stairs. "You've been dismissed by my lady and ain't wanted in this house," he said and slammed the door.

I sat heavily on the bottom step. My head swam. Somehow, I'd become my maid. Then I remembered the crone, Eliza, and the singing bowl. I'd been on my deathbed, barely alive. Mother must have summoned the witch to save me. But I had not been saved. I'd been transported into the body of my maid. Had Abby died in my stead? Did my mother not understand I, or that my soul at least, now resided inside Abby? And what happened to my real body? Was I dead? Was I still lying on my bed struggling for each breath? And why had Chadwick said I was dismissed? Why would my mother send Abby away if she knew her daughter's spirit resided inside Abby? Nothing made any sense. And where was I supposed to go? What was I supposed to do?

The door opened again and I scrambled to hide in a dark corner beside the stairs. Eliza stepped out and the door slammed shut behind her. In the light of the lamp, I saw the ancient crone carried a large satchel. It bulged with the singing bowl. I must get it. If my real body still lived, if infusing it with Abby's spirit healed it, I would need the bowl to return to my body. How would I live as Abby? I had no home now as I'd been dismissed, no references with which to apply for another job. Terror at the thought of what could happen to a young girl on the street filled me.

Eliza left the house and turned onto Halfmoon Street heading toward Piccadilly. "Eliza!" I called.

The crone turned, looked at me, and cackled. "Not so high and mighty now, are ye?"

"You must change me back," I cried. "You must."

Eliza's wrinkled face beamed with pleasure. "I done what yer ma wanted. I healed yer body. She didn't say nothing about yer soul cause she don't be caring. All she wants is gold and the Bleakstone diamonds. She don't care about you or naught else."

I grabbed for her hand and she snatched it away as though I was a leper. "Please. Where will I go? What will I do?"

"Maybe you should ask yer ma. Oh wait, ye cain't cause you be only a maid." She cackled and continued walking.

I trailed her, filled with fear, cold, shivering, and desperate. This was the only thing I could think to do. I caught up with her and grabbed her shoulder. "You can't leave me like this."

"Can and will." We'd reached Piccadilly where Eliza summoned a hack. She glanced back at me. "Get yerself and yer old body to Bleak House, right the wrongs done by yer ma, and I might change you back. But she needs to be there, too, cause she be the only one who know where it's hidden. She's the only one who knows where my Julia is. Bitch!" She spat the last word then climbed into the hack and headed toward the East End. As I watched the horse-drawn hack trot away, all hope seeped out of me. I fell to the pavers sobbing. What was I to do now? I couldn't get all the way to Bleak House. It was miles away in Codford near Dorset. And what could Mother have hidden and how was I to get her to Bleak House a place to which she'd sworn never to return?

I turned back the way I'd come and walked down Halfmoon Street, my shoulders hunched against the sudden downpour of cold rain, my arms wrapped around my body. They hadn't even given me a coat or my clothes when they threw me out. I was freezing. A sharp hiss from an alley between houses caught my attention. "What?"

"Abby, it's me Drusilla Washburn from Lady Amberfield's."

I stared into the dark alley. A slim maid dressed in a dark blue gown covered with a black cloak beckoned to me from the shadows. "Drusilla?" When Abby had attended Lilianna on her visits to Lady Amberfield's daughter, Claire, Abby often disappeared into the servants' quarters. I remembered Claire's maid was named Drusilla."

"What be you a doing out this late?" Drusilla asked.

"I was dismissed, thrown out without even my clothes," I cried. "I don't even know why."

Drusilla wrapped her arm around me. "You be about freezing to death. Come with me. You can sleep in me room on the trundle bed. Tomorrow I'll talk to the housekeeper, Mrs. Whimsey, about getting you placed with the Amberfields. I can't believe Lady Everleigh would throw you out. Why it's downright inhuman, it is."

She led me in through the servants' entrance of the Amberfield mansion and down the stairs to the servants' quarters. There was no fire in Drusilla's room, but it was warm from the big, closed stove in the kitchens which were close to her room. She sat me on the bed and wrapped a wool blanket around me. "I'll get you a hot cup a tea. That'll fix you right up."

How could Drusilla know nothing would fix me? I wasn't Abby, I was Lilianna. I had no idea what was going to happen to me. All I did know was I had to get to Eliza. She said I should go to Bleak House which was close to Codford. Mother's family came from there. Bleak House was a huge pile, damp and dark, on the Wylye River outside of Codford St. Mary. I'd visited the house as a child when Mother's father was still alive. Old Lord Bleakestone was a horrible man who'd reeked of snuff and pomade when he'd pinched my cheeks. After he died, Mother's older brother, Everard Smythe, the new Lord Bleakestone, inherited. Mother never got on with Uncle Everard's new wife, so we ceased visiting which was no hardship for me because the huge ugly house was frightening and uncomfortable. Had Eliza gone home to Codford? I dropped my head into my hands. How could I follow her there? I had no money. I was destitute.

I slept on the trundle bed and was awakened very early by pans banging in the nearby kitchen. Drusilla poked me. "Get up and do something with yer hair. You look like ye been dragged through a bush backward. Mrs. Whimsey be in her office above stairs." Drusilla opened a trunk and removed a plain blue wool dress like the one she wore. "Here, put this on. Yer dress be muddied and bedaubed with horse leavings." She shook out the dress and handed it to me. "I have to attend to Miss Claire later, but she ain't likely to wake until noon. Give me plenty of time to take you to see Mrs. Whimsey. She's a strict one, she is, but fair. And I know we be needin' a scullery maid. Last one piked on the bean Thursday week and the upstairs maid's had to wash the pots and dishes. She ain't happy."

Scullery maid? Horrified, I scrambled into the blue dress. Drusilla had been right. The black one Abby, or me now, had been wearing was disgustingly filthy. I had no right to complain, but scullery maid? Tears ran down my face.

What had Mother done so long ago to anger Eliza, and how could I find out what it was and drag Mother all the way to Codford St. Mary?

Chapter Three

I worked as the Amberfield's scullery maid for two weeks. I got up earlier than any of the other servants and started the fire in the massive, closed stove and the fireplace for the spits. Then I scrubbed pots, pans, and over and over the kitchen floor. After meals, I washed dishes and utensils, hauled hot water to and from the big sinks, dried and put away the dishes, and scrubbed the floor. At night, I fell into bed exhausted. I had no time to think about Lilianna, Eliza, my mother or how I was to return to my body. I had plenty of time to reflect on the horrors of being a scullery maid and how I would work to change things if I were ever given the opportunity.

One day Drusilla got me from my sinks and pulled me aside. "Lilianna be visiting," she whispered. "Would you be wishing to see her? Mayhap ask why ye were dismissed?'

So, Lilianna, I, had survived. The old witch's spell or her magic bowl had saved her. I dried my dripping hands on a clean towel. "Yes, I would like to see her if it can be arranged."

"When she gets ready to leave, I'll take you to the hall. She'll be putting on her cloak and gathering her muff. John, the butler, said he'd let me know."

My heart raced. What would I say? I'd be speaking to my maid who was probably quite happy as Lilianna and no doubt reluctant to return to what I now knew was virtual slavery as a servant. When Drusilla grabbed my hand and dragged me down several corridors and into the hall I almost backed out. Only the thought of the endless drudgery ahead of me in the Amberfield's kitchens kept me moving.

Drusilla opened the door at the end of the corridor and shoved me through. There she was . . . Lilianna, me, only not me anymore. She wore my best morning gown of pommona-green twilled silk. She held her arms out for the butler to help her into my dark-green pelisse tied with silk ribbons of a lighter green. As she placed my favorite bonnet on her head of blond curls, I ground my teeth and stepped in front of her. She gasped and grabbed her throat. "You!"

"Enjoying yourself, my lady?" I snarled.

She backed two steps running right into the butler. "I had no idea this would happen," she squeaked. "I thought I would be the one dying, and you would live."

"You seem comfortable in my body, living my life. Does my mother know?"

She who was really Abby grabbed the front of my damp apron with both hands. "Your mother knows everything. She knew what would happen. She knew you would go into my body and she didn't care as long as Lilianna's body survived. She's possessed by the idea of marrying you to a duke to save your father and her from the poor house. She's a monster."

I gasped. "My own mother threw me out into the street without even a coat?"

"Yes," Abby whispered. "Yes. She didn't want anyone getting even a sniff of what had actually happened. She cooked up this plan with the witch, Eliza. Eliza did it to get something from your mother, something your mother has kept secret for years, something Eliza values above all else in this world. And Eliza is doing something for yer mother. I don't know what it is."

"Eliza lied to me. She said Mother didn't know. She did tell me whatever Mother is hiding is at Bleak House."

Abby closed her eyes. My eyes. "Oh, she knew. She's been teaching me to speak proper English, table manners, how to simper and flirt." Abby stripped off a glove and showed me the back of her hand. It was black and purple with bruises. "She hits me with a yardstick when I make mistakes. She pinches me most cruelly. I have more bruises under these fine clothes."

Abby had been with me since we were both small children. We'd grown up together as sisters. Now, of course, I knew her life had been very different from mine. While she toiled from sunup to sunset, sometimes long after waiting on me, I'd known indolence and luxury. "I'm so sorry," I wailed. "I never knew how hard your life was."

She grabbed me and we hugged. "I was content with my lot in life. I never wished for more. I love you as a sister. How can we fix this? We must. I can't go on pretending to be you and I hate your mother. She's selfish and cruel. Why, I believe she'd kill me if I refused to do her bidding, and the pretending is making me crazy. Between your mother's cruelty and trying to be something I wasn't born to and never wished for, I be about ready for the lunatic asylum."

Drusilla grabbed my arm. "I got no idea what be happening here. There's something strange going on betwixt the two of ye, that's for certain. I don't understand and I'm scared to. But we can't be seen like this in the hall. Servants talk." She glanced around nervously. "The library. No one's there cause Lord Amberfield is at his club and Gordon is up to Oxford." We followed her down the hall to a set of double doors. She glanced quickly up and down the empty hall, then drew us into the library.

Abby who was me, Lilianna, grabbed me again and hugged me. "That old witch cured ye sure enough, but to do it she had to do this, and yer mam knew it when she called on her and she didn't care as long as yer body survived to do what she wants. It's horrible. I'm supposed to go to a rout party tonight and dance. I don't know how to dance, and I'm scared down to me shoes. There's an old Duke whose wife just died. He's in his sixties. Yer ma introduced us at a dinner party last night and I'm sure she intends to sell me to him. He's rich and fat and disgusting. He drooled all over my hand."

"Eliza went back to Bleak House," I said. "My uncle is bedridden with some mysterious ailment and Aunt Lucretia plans to come to London for the season."

"Well yer ma says Eliza is the housekeeper. While yer aunt is gone, Eliza is in charge and your Uncle Everard has no idea what she be doing. I can't say whether Eliza is truly the evil one. Yer ma done something terrible to her long ago and Eliza wants it fixed."

"If Eliza is at Bleak House, then we need to go there and get her to change us back," I said. "And somehow I need Mother to be there and give Eliza whatever she's keeping hidden."

"Yer ma barely lets me out of her sight. She's on her way right now to pick me up. She sent me here to speak to Claire about getting invited to the ball at Clively House. This horrible Duke of Rushford who yer ma wants to sell me to will be there." Abby sobbed into her handkerchief. "My poor Jack is probably beside hisself with worry."

"Who is Jack?" I asked.

"My fiancé," Abby said. "We was planning to get hitched when you went to Bath for the summer."

I felt horrible. Abby had a fiancé and I had never known about it. "I'm so sorry," I cried. "I was a terrible mistress. I know nothing of your personal life." I covered my eyes with my hands in shame. Abby pulled my hands away. "You was always kind to me. Yer the best mistress out of all the fine ladies who's maids I've ever met."

"We have to go to Bleak House. And we must bring Mother. But how are we to manage this with me here and you being watched?"

"I found Frederick's money stash. He'd been gambling and hiding his money from yer ma. She's horrible tight-fisted and woulda taken it to pay your father's gambling debts. We can use the money to take the stage to Dorset."

I brightened. "I can believe Freddy gambles, but that he wins? I find that a stretch, but I am profoundly grateful he has done so. As brothers go, he hasn't ever been a bad one, often sheltering me from Mother's wrath. If we can get to Dorset, we can borrow or rent a gig from and inn or livery stable to drive out to Bleak House."

Abby gasped. "I can't drive no gig."

"Well I can."

"I don't know how I can get out of the house. Yer ma watches my every move. She locks me in your room at night."

"You'll have to be very quiet, but you can sneak out through the dressing room. There's a secret door behind my dresses. I found it when I was a child. It leads to the scullery." I shivered. "A place I'm now very much more familiar with."

The doorbell peeled and Abby jumped. "I know it's her. She's come fer me."

The Amberfield footman opened the library door. "Lady Everleigh has come for her daughter."

Suddenly, my mother appeared behind the footman. "What could Lilianna possibly be doing in the library?" She demanded of the footman. When she saw me, her eyes narrowed. "You!" She grabbed the footman's arm. "Call the watch immediately and have him arrest this common thief. I fired her for stealing my jewelry. Get her!"

Confused, the footman froze, and Abby grabbed my arm. "Run," she screamed and dragged me straight at my mother. Together, we pushed my mother and the shocked footman aside, and bolted out the open front door into the street.

Chapter Four

It was raining again. Late February in London is dreary and cold. Soon the Season would begin, and the empty houses would be filled with parties and gaiety. But now, few homes were occupied, and it was horribly cold.

Abby grabbed my hand. "Run fast. We have to get to your house, get inside and get Frederick's money before yer mam gets back."

We raced through the pouring rain. There was no time to worry about being wet or cold. We had to get there before she did. When we got to my house, she dragged me right into the front door. I hung back at first, remembering my last encounter with the footman. She pulled harder. "I'm Lilianna. I can do anything. Come on."

We entered the front hall, she lifted her long skirts, raced up the stairs to the first floor, and then went right up the second staircase to Freddie's room. Abby swept her skirts aside, dropped to her knees close to the bed, removed a section of the baseboard, and pulled out a pouch filled with money. "Yer ma had me cleaning the baseboards while Freddie was up to Oxford. That's how I found this."

I lifted the pouch. It was heavy. "How much is in here?"

"I never counted, and it looks like he's added some more. I just hope it's enough to get us to Codford and Bleak House."

We ran to my room where Abby stuffed garments, brushes, night clothes and caps into a valise. She handed me a warm cloak. "Put this on." She threw the green pelisse aside and grabbed another heavy cloak shrugging into it. "Let's go."

At that very moment, we heard a commotion in the front hall. "Is that wench here?" My mother screamed.

As much as it pained me to know my mother wanted me gone forever, I had to ignore it. "This way," I said to Abby and led her back into my room, through the dressing room, a narrow door hidden behind my ball gowns, and down a steep set of steps. We exited in the scullery. Cissy the scullery maid screamed when she saw us, and Abby hushed her. She dragged me out the servants exit and into a dark, stinking alley. We ran behind our house into an side street that led behind all the big houses on Curzon. When she finally stopped running, I was gasping for breath.

"Where can we catch the Mail to Dorset? Or the stage or something?"

I had to stop and think. "The Mail leaves from the Central Letter Office. I know it goes to

Dorset but I don't know when. Let's get on the first coach we can and just get out of London."

"Where is the letter office?" Abby asked.

I waved my hand. "Close to St. Paul's Cathedral. We'll get a hack. The jarvey will know."

"There they are!" It was my mother. She was shrieking. "Get Lilianna. Don't let her get away."

Abby grabbed my hand and we took off running again. This time toward Piccadilly. "We can get a hack near the park," I gasped remembering Eliza had found one there.

Abby glanced behind. "She's got Lichfield after us. He's young and can run."

"Oh no, hurry."

She grabbed my hand and jerked me into a dark alley off Halfmoon Street. We ran between two houses, out the back and down the alley in the direction of Piccadilly. When we popped out on the sidewalk, there was a hack parked at the curb right in front of us. Abby yanked open the door of the carriage. "Central Mail please," she told the driver.

"Stop!" My father's groom, Lichfield yelled. "Don't let them get away."

Abby threw back her shoulders and shoved me into the carriage. She pointed at Lichfield. "He accosted me and now he wants to rob us. My maid and I need to go to St. Paul's. Are you going to take us or not?" She waved a golden coin around in two gloved fingers. The jarvey pulled his forelock, snatched the coin, and pointed to the carriage door. Abby climbed in after me and the driver slammed the door.

Lichfield tried accosting him, but the agile jarvey leaped onto his box and whipped up the horse. We set off at a spanking trot leaving Lichfield behind.

I fell back against the seat and Abby patted my hand. "Try not to worry so much, Miss. We got plenty of money and we're safe now."

"The best part of all this is my mother will take a mere minute to figure out where we are going, and she will come after us. I know it. I will be doing as Eliza instructed; coming to Bleak House and bringing my mother with me."

Abby nodded. "Reckon she will, but we'll have to stay ahead of her, or she'll drag me back and then it will be the duke fer me and goal fer you. I have no doubt she'll lock you up to save herself." She shuddered with horror.

We had to wait until the Mail loaded and left. Two agonizing hours sitting on a bench in front of the huge building fearing Mother would show up at any moment. We boarded the crowded Mail coach and were finally leaving London headed toward Bath. The man who sold us the tickets said we must alight in

Hungerford and catch a Stage to Salisbury. The man said it would let us off at the Ox Bow Inn where we could rent a tilbury or a gig to Codford some thirteen miles away.

I was exhausted and squashed between a large woman with a rush basket on her lap and Abby. Abby had the seat next to the window because of her station. She was Lilianna Everleigh. I was the maid. It didn't matter to me where I sat. I fell deeply asleep before we were out of London.

The Mail pulled into Hungerford in the early-morning hours. It was dark. Abby and I tottered into the inn carrying our one valise and discovered the Stage was leaving in less than ten minutes for Salisbury. I was so glad. The Stage was not as crowded as the Mail had been. We had room to sit in comfort. The eight-hour ride to Salisbury went fast and soon we were alighting at the Ox Bow Inn. It was almost five o'clock. I looked at Abby as droopy and exhausted as I was. "Let's stay the night here and set off for Codford first thing in the morning."

Abby nodded and we went looking for the landlord. He took one look at Abby and began bowing and scraping. We were given one room with a big bed and a truckle bed set up in the dressing room, probably for me. We had a private parlor where we dined on a substantial meal. After eating, Abby was going to lie down on the truckle bed, but I insisted she share the big bed with me. "Abby, you are as my sister. We've shared everything. Now we even have shared bodies. You are me and I am you. Climb in."

After we washed our faces and donned the night gear Abby had packed, she insisted on combing out my hair and fitting my cap. Over her protests, I combed her hair, hair that used to be mine, and stuck the spare nightcap on her head. We laughed as we fell into the bed and slept awaking to the sound of a groom calling for a change of horses. I was horrified when I recognized the voice. "It's Lichfield. Mother must have figured out we are going to Bleak House and she's following as we expected. I'd just hoped we'd have a little more time."

We dressed and ran down the back stairs and out into the stable yard behind the inn. Abby carried the valise. As soon as I spotted the innkeeper, I snatched it away from her. "You can't be seen carrying luggage for the maid. Now go speak to the innkeeper and ask if there is a curricle or another form of conveyance we can rent."

"I couldn't," Abby said. "I'm only a maid."

I grabbed her shoulders. "Abby, you are now Lilianna Everleigh. You must speak to the landlord. I cannot. He will think it beyond odd if the maid does the talking."

Abby squared her shoulders and resolutely walked up to the landlord. A gig pulled in behind the landlord and stopped. A young man jumped down and tossed the reins to the hostler. He waved to the landlord and ran into the inn. I stepped close to Abby to listen to her conversation with the innkeeper. "Sir," she began, and I cringed. Fine ladies did not address innkeepers as sir. "I would like to hire a curricle or a small conveyance such as that one. Is there one available?"

He pulled his forelock but gave her a strange look. "No, miss, we be having no extra carts or carriages here today. There's a sporting event in the next town and all been rented by fine gentlemen wishing to watch. Now tomorrow, we'll have several for you to choose from."

By sporting event, I assumed he meant a boxing match. Abby quailed. I heard Lichfield shouting from inside the inn. He was ordering a servant to bring tea and breakfast to one of the parlors. It must mean Mother was in there. Panic filled me and I grabbed Abby's hand. She looked at me, saw the panic and began to cry. The innkeeper patted her hand. "Don't worry, Miss, just go inside and I'll have my wife make you a cup of tea. You can stay an extra night and leave in the morning fine as five pence."

I squeezed Abby's hand. She gulped and smiled at the landlord. When he bowed and walked toward the inn, I shoved Abby toward the gig. The hostler was still holding the horse's reins. I swished toward him and put on my best saucy maid face. "Can I hold the reins for a moment?" I asked in a seductive voice. "He's such a beautiful horse and I do love them."

The horse was old, sway backed, and asleep with one foot cocked. But the hostler was blinded by my smile and handed me the reins. "Get in," I yelled to Abby, scrambled onto the seat before the stunned hostler could realize he'd been diddled, and gathered my reins. "Toss the hostler a coin. Make him chase it," I said.

Abby threw a gold sovereign a good distance as I clucked to the horse and turned him in the tight space. Once pointed out of the yard, the ancient nag picked up a slow shuffle and off we went.

"This horse is so slow, your mother could catch us walking," Abby said.

"I know a back road. It's nothing but a narrow cart track. I'm sure this gig and the ancient horse can make it, but I doubt if Mother either knows of it or could get her traveling chaise down it. We just need to get to the turn off."

I felt bad pushing the ancient gelding, but we were desperate. I cracked the whip over his head, and he broke into an awkward canter. His jarring gait had us jolting and rocking but I soon saw the signpost for Codford St. Mary and the narrow lane that turned off right before it. I slowed the horse and made the tight turn onto the lane. In minutes, we were lost inside two lines of thick trees edging fields of winter rye. I slowed the horse and let him walk. Poor old gentleman.

"This is a shortcut," I told Abby who clutched her seat with a white face.

"Miss Lilianna," she said in a breathless voice. "I was sure you'd turn us over."

"I'm a much better horsewoman than that. Let us pray we arrive at Bleak House before Mother."

"What about the young man? We just stole his gig and his horse."

"I feel sure he'll be upset, but there's nothing we can do. We must get to Bleak House. Our lives depend on it, Abby. This is no small matter."

"I know," she said. "I know."

Chapter Five

When we finally arrived at the entrance to Bleak House, the poor gelding in the shafts was about done for. I turned him into the drive. This time of year, bare branches like ghostly fingers hung over the road. It seemed as though they reached for us. The drive was long, but soon we spotted the old mansion. It had been built in the time of Charles II, constructed in the Victorian Gothic style with several towers and a multitude of pointed, arched windows. The stone was darkened from years of neglect and the windows dirty, but on the very top floor a light flickered in the window and a shadow flitted in front of the light.

Abby pointed. "I saw a light."

I nodded. "I did, too, but I can't imagine why anyone would be up in the attics."

Ivy climbed up the north side of the house covering the windows on that side. Several large oaks hung twisted branches over the gardens which were overgrown with weeds and small bare-branched shrubs. To top off this dreary scene, it began to drizzle, and a stiff wind whipped the gelding's mane. Abby snatched at her bonnet to keep it from being carried away.

"That is an ugly old house," Abby said. "It looks haunted."

"It is," I returned. "By Eliza."

"If it looks like this outside, what's it like inside?"

"Worse. There's a priest hole, a multitude of dark passages with rotting floors and moldy wainscoting. Every fireplace in the house smokes profusely when the wind is in the east which it almost always is, and there is a cellar that runs deep and is said to have several sub-cellars. I never went down there. I was too little. Mother said her brother never employs enough staff because he's a terrible nip-farthing, so the food is usually served cold in the vast dining hall. Staying here is always an uncomfortable experience. Mother ceased visiting when I was a small child, so I have not been here in quite some time. When I was small, feelings of dread used to fill me at night, and I heard strange moaning noises coming from the attics. I tried to crawl into bed with Mother, but she made me go back to my own room. I swear, I rarely slept a wink while we were here."

Abby shuddered. "We need to get that bowl, get changed back, and get out of here as fast as possible."

I drove the gig into the stable yard which appeared to be deserted. Abby hopped down and so did I. The stables were in a U shape, many of them falling apart, the stalls empty. One section seemed to be in use. I took the reins and led the tired horse under a covered space between the first and second sections. "We can't just abandon this old guy here," I told Abby. "Help me remove his harness."

We'd just taken the harness off the horse and tied it to a hook in the wall when an old man appeared. He walked around the gig. "Who be ye?" He asked.

I nudged Abby. "I am Lilianna Everleigh come to visit my uncle."

"Well he ain't expecting no visitors."

The sun had set, and long shadows stretched across the yard. I pinched Abby's arm and she spoke to the old man. "My mother is following and will soon arrive. Are you the groom?"

The old man cackled. "I be groom, butler, and general man about the house," he said.

I handed Abby the lead rope and she thrust it at the old man. "Then please brush and tend to this animal. I must go inside and find my uncle."

"Eliza be mistress here now," the old man said. "I'm thinkin' she be in the front hall waitin' fer ye. Dark doings been going on since she arrived, but the master won't hear nothing agin her. Bleak House weren't no paradise before she come. Now, it's downright scary. But the master thinks he's had his notice to quit and don't seem to care for nothing but his dinner which that witch Eliza fixes special fer him. Poisoning him is what I think. Poisoning his body and his mind."

I grabbed Abby's hand and we left the old man with the horse to care for. As we walked toward the front door, Abby hissed in my ear. "If Eliza is in charge, we're in deep trouble, Miss. What do we do?"

"I doubt if Eliza will harm us in my uncle's home. We need her to change us back. She's the only one who can. If she won't, we must steal that bowl and do it ourselves."

Abby's only answer was a whimper of fear as she clutched my hand even more tightly. We walked down a narrow path between tall oaks that swayed in the wind. A sharp crack split the air and a huge branch dropped right in front of us. Abbey squealed and clutched me. We stepped around the downed limb and walked faster. It seemed as though we were being chased. I kept glancing behind but no one or anything else was there.

When we reached the porte-cochere, and climbed the stairs, we didn't have to ring the bell of knock, when we got close to the big double entrance doors, they swung open and Eliza stood in the center of the hall dressed all in black with her hands held out in front of her.

"Why are you two here?" She demanded. "Yer ma ain't with you. She knows what she's kept from me. She knows what I want. No way I'm switchin' you back until I get it." Lightning issued from her raised hands, a loud bang echoed off the stone walls, and smoke filled the huge hall. Abby squealed and clutched my arm. I stood firm. When the smoke cleared, Eliza was gone.

"Come on," I said to Abby. "We must try to find my uncle. Perhaps he will know where Eliza sleeps or where she has disappeared to."

The house was dark. Night had fallen. The wind dragged the ivy vines back and forth across the north wall making scratching noises like ghostly fingers on rock. I spotted a lamp burning down a long corridor I thought led to the kitchens and followed it. Abby hung back. "This can't be good. Why it feels like a trap. No other lights, suddenly a lamp, it's like they be teasing us."

"If it is a trap. It's a good one, because we have no way to light even a candle. We must follow the lamp."

The stone corridor did indeed lead to the kitchens. The lamp turned out to be held by the old groom. He set it on a trestle table and stoked up the fire in the open stove. An old woman wearing a faded gray gown covered with a black apron stooped as she lifted a pot of stew off the hob and set it onto the stove. She glanced at Abby and me and frowned. "Ye got no business being here. It's a dangerous place."

"We must find Eliza," I said. "She disappeared."

"You don't want to find her, believe you me. She's an evil one, she is. Killing the master slowly. We just don't know how to stop her."

"Who else is here beside you two and Uncle Everard?" I asked.

"What's wrong with Miss Lilianna?" The old woman asked. "Can't she speak?"

"Eliza switched me with my maid," I told her. "I'm Lilianna. Who are you? Should I remember you?"

"I'm Mrs. Beetles and this is my husband, Clarence Beetles. We worked here at Bleak House most of our lives. I remember you as a toddler and then when you were about six or so. Last time yer ma came here, Mr. Everard had just married that trollop, Harriet Arbuthnot, and yer ma took and got into a right nasty brangle with her over some furniture and the Bleakstone diamonds. Though the diamonds ain't no business of yer ma's. They belong to the heir and that be Master Everard."

"I know nothing of my mother and the diamonds, but she is coming here, that I can assure you. She and her groom, Lichfield, are on their way."

A noise such as slow footsteps came from the hallway behind me and I whirled around. It was Eliza holding a candle. She wore a black dress buttoned up to her chin with long black sleeves. We stood like statues as she set the candle on the kitchen table.

"Augusta be coming here cause she knows she has to. This is the time to end what she started. This is the time for her to give me back my child."

"I don't understand," I said. "What is happening?"

Eliza stared at me through her glittering black eyes. "Yer ma got herself a dresser, a personal maid named Jane. Right?"

I nodded. "She's had Jane with her since she was twelve. Jane is now her dresser. She must be about five years older than me. Mother keeps her very close. I don't think I've spoken above five words with her in all the time she's been with Mother."

"Been longer than that," Eliza said. "She took Jane when the child was only eight. You should remember playing with her when you were little."

I did remember a child, older than me but pretty, who led me around the gardens and played tag, duck, duck, goose, and spillikins with me. "Yes, I remember now."

"I had a child then, Julia. She was sixteen and so lovely. She got sick. I worked in the village as a seamstress, but everyone knew I had me some other powers I learnt from me ma who was a gypsy. I had the bowl. Yer ma was here at the house visiting. Her pa had just died, and Augusta wanted the Bleakstone diamonds even though she knew they was Everard's and Everard was planning to marry. He refused to give them up, so yer ma came to me. She installed me here as housekeeper and offered Jane to me to save me daughter."

"I'm confused," I said. "Did you save your daughter? What happened?"

Me daughter is lying in the deepest cellars asleep forever or at least until yer ma gives me the key to the cellar she's locked in and brings Jane to me. She's refused to do that until she gets the diamonds. She wants me to kill Everard. He has no heir so Augusta will get the diamonds. Without the key and Jane, I can't bring Julia back. I don't even know which of the cellar chambers Julia be in."

"Jane is Julia, isn't she?" I asked.

Eliza nodded.

"The bowl? But why is the girl in the cellars sleeping? Why doesn't she wake up?"

"Julia was sick unto death. She was in a coma when I went to yer ma. I had to put her in a permanent state of sleep to save her. We used the bowl to transfer their souls. We did it in the cellars to keep it all secret. I woulda woke her up when Julia was in Jane's body, but yer ma had that man Lichfield knock me down and carry me away. Then she locked the door of the cellar and put me here as housekeeper."

A sudden commotion from the front hall startled all of us out of the shocked lethargy listening to Eliza had induced. I jumped. "Mother!"

"She's come for me," Abby wailed.

"Sure she has," Eliza said. "But if she wants you, she better have Jane with her and the key." Eliza grabbed Abby's arm and took off running for the scullery. I followed, wringing my hands. After Eliza's story, Mother was an even more terrifying figure. It seemed she'd do anything if it served her purpose and her purpose was to obtain the Bleakstone diamonds and Abby as Lilianna.

Eliza entered a tiny door in the back of one of the pantries. It went up a series of staircases with tall, narrow steps, that exited in the attics. Once in the attics, I saw why we'd seen a light in the filthy window when we were walking toward the house. Uncle Everard lay on a bed looking pale and wan but very much alive. Eliza shoved Abby toward a cupboard and me with her. "Hide here. Yer ma don't know the way up to this attic. No one does save me. I been trying to keep Lord Bleakstone alive. The Beetles are the ones trying to kill him. Paid by yer ma."

I gasped. "But they said it was you trying to kill him."

"No," Eliza said. "That wouldn't do me a bit of good. I need Lord Bleakstone alive to use as a bargaining chip with yer ma. I told him the whole and he's given me the diamonds so I can get my Julia back. He sent his wife to London cause I knew it were time to end this."

I gently pushed Eliza aside and went to my uncle's bedside. "I'm sorry for what my mother is doing. Believe me, I had no part in it."

"You are not Lilianna," Uncle Everard said in a weak voice.

"Yes, Uncle, I am Lilianna. Eliza put me in this body because I had consumption and was dying of an inflammation of my lungs. It saved me, but now I am my maid and my maid is in my body. We came here to get Eliza to change us back and found all of this." I waved my hand to indicate the house and Eliza. "My mother is so evil."

He nodded and lifted his hand which I grasped in mine. "She must be destroyed before she can do more evil. I fear she will stop at nothing to get her way."

Eliza pushed me toward the cupboard. "Stay hidden until I come to get you. Your mother must give me back my daughter before I give her anything."

I shook my head. "No, I will go with you. Abby is the one who must stay hidden. I wish to confront my mother. Hiding will fix nothing."

"As you wish," Eliza snarled. "But I warned ye."

We left poor Abby huddled in the cupboard, raced down the steps, slipped out of the pantry, and ran into the kitchens. Lichfield was there. "You!" He said. "Where's the other one, Lilianna?"

"Where you will never find her."

"Lichfield, Lichfield," my mother called from the hall. "Bring me a branch of candles. It's as dark as the dungeons in here."

Lichfield lit a large branch of candles and headed toward the main hall. Eliza and I followed. Mother stood in the hall, tall and regal. Jane hovered behind her. "You," she said with loathing dripping from her voice. "Where is my daughter?"

"I am your daughter, and well you know it. We have hidden Abby and you shall not have her."

"Are you ready to give me back my Julia?" Eliza asked.

"Not until I get those diamonds."

"I have the Bleakstone diamonds, but you'll not have them until I get the key and you take me to the chamber where my Julia lies sleeping."

Mother's eyes narrowed as her face took on a crafty expression. "How can I be sure you won't diddle me. I want those diamonds and I want my daughter."

"Give me the key and ye shall have the cursed diamonds. But you must take me into the cellars and show me the chamber before I give you Lilianna."

Mother opened a locket hanging on a chain around her neck. I had seen it many times. She'd told me it contained miniatures of her parents but would never show me their portraits. She removed a key and held it close to her body. "The key."

Eliza reached into one of the capacious pockets in her skirt and pulled a necklace of enormous diamonds out of it. Mother's eyes gleamed when she saw the necklace. "The Bleakstone diamonds. Give them to me."

"Not so fast," Eliza said. "We be going into the cellars to make sure this key you have actually opens the chamber where my daughter lies."

"Lichfield, get them!" Mother screeched.

Eliza pointed a long bony finger at Lichfield, and he ignited in a blazing pyre. Lichfield's screams of agony filled the hall. "Stop the flames!" Mother screamed. "Lichfield. Lichfield."

I backed away with my hand covering my mouth to contain my screams. Horror gripped my heart in a vice of terror as Lichfield's flesh sizzled and the fat from his body fed the flames and dripped onto the flagstones. Jane shrieked and turned to run. Mother whirled and grabbed her maid by her hair. "Oh, no you don't," she snarled.

"Yer precious groom's done fer," Eliza said as Lichfield fell to the floor and the screams died. The flames burned hot, blue-white and orange as he lay on the stones writhing in agony until suddenly the flames went out and all that was left of Lichfield was a pile of ash. "If you'd like to join him, take me to the wrong chamber," Eliza said. "My powers have grown since you stole my child. I can fry you with one word."

Chapter Six

We trouped through the kitchens as a group, walked past the Beetles who stood frozen, staring at us as though we were devils. I couldn't believe they were the ones slowly poisoning Uncle Everard, and I still had my doubts about Eliza, but I did know Mother was evil and Eliza had her reasons for what she did. That Mother wanted Uncle dead, I easily believed. I'd seen her eyes glow when she spotted the diamonds. Even now, she inched closer and closer to Eliza as we entered the stairs going down to the dark cellars. Her hands were clenched into claws and I could see them twitching as though she yearned to snatch the necklace from Eliza's pocket.

Eliza ignited a torch by pointing her finger at it. She lit a second torch and handed it to me. "You, walk behind to light yer mam." She pushed Mother to the front when we hit a landing. "Which room is my Julia in? Lead us."

We exited the long stone staircase into a dark hall with an arched ceiling. It was cold and damp. I shivered with terror as Mother stood in the center of the hall and looked around. Doors with barred windows lined this hallway which looked like a dungeon and may have been one long ago. "Not on this floor," Mother said. "Lower."

She opened one door, wood with long, beaten-metal hinges, to reveal another set of stairs, these narrow with a low ceiling. The steps, a foot tall, seemed carved from the bedrock upon which Bleak House had been built. "Go on," Eliza said. "Move."

Mother seemed hesitant. "There's evil demons down there," she finally said. "They've lived here for generations and they hate all of the Bleakstone family. Ghosts of the long dead. Tortured souls who died in the dungeons and at the hands of our ancestors. They hate us and they guard your daughter."

Eliza laughed as she pushed Jane toward Mother. "Good, you two go first." She turned to me. "Have a care Lilianna. Your mother's evil is probably connected to these demons, but I been down here afore and never found my Julia or no ghosts."

Mother growled but carefully descended. The steps seemed to go into the very bowels of the earth. We went by a door. Mother briefly stopped her descent. "Wine cellars," she said, turned and continued down.

I felt as though the staircase had no end. It finally stopped at another of those wooden doors. The door looked primitive, crudely constructed of planks nailed together with hand-made spikes. Mother opened it by lifting a bar that creaked and groaned. All the hair on my arms rose. My scalp crawled and I filled with terrible fear. Jane began to weep. "Please don't take me in there. Please."

Eliza then did a strange thing. She wrapped her arms around Jane. "You are my Julia. Do not fear. Soon, you will be with me again and in your rightful body." She patted another pocket in her skirt and for the first time, I saw the tell-tale bulge of the singing bowl.

Jane shrugged off Eliza's arm. "I don't want to be anyone else. I don't know you."

Eliza's face registered hurt. "Yet, ye are my daughter and I know you."

The corridor on the other side of the door was more a tunnel in a cave than a hallway. The walls still bore the marks of the tools used to carve it from the rock. Mother walked slowly as a cold wind blew through my hair and the temperature dropped. I wrapped my hands around my body and shivered. Eliza made the sign of the cross and mumbled words in Latin. Mother suddenly screamed and batted at her face. "Get away!" she yelled.

Eliza shoved Jane toward me and pushed Mother in the back. "Move, bitch. I ain't buying your fear or your crazed actions. Ye be fakin'."

"No!" Mother screamed again and began batting at her clothes. I saw her skirts lifted, her legs encased in silk stockings were revealed. Her blouse was torn away. She screamed and screamed as moaning and groaning issued from the walls. Blood ran down the rocks, glistening and red in the light of the torches. Eliza grabbed Mother. "Give me the key and show me which room and you can run away. If you don't, these demons who hate you Bleakstones will kill you."

"There, that room." Mother pointed to a door at the end of the passage as her skirts were ripped away and claw marks raked her face and down her shoulders. Blood dripped from the scratches and she threw the key at Eliza. "Let me go!" she screamed. "Give me my diamonds."

Jane fell to the floor weeping hysterically as Mother's shift was torn off. Her naked breasts were scored with more claw marks. Her undergarments were ripped away and she stood as God had made her, her white skin glowing, red blood flowing in the light from the torch she'd dropped to the dirt floor.

Eliza ignored her and scooped Jane up. "Come with me, girl, unless you wish to receive the same treatment as your mistress."

"Mother," I said with tears running down my face. I reached for her, but she was shrouded in a cocoon of ice. She writhed in agony as had Lichfield, he in fire, her in ice. I couldn't save her. I couldn't touch her. She'd treated me with scorn and no love, but still, she was my mother.

"Bring the torch," Eliza ordered me. I glanced once more at Mother, whose shrieks had ceased, then stepped around her. Eliza carried the torch Mother had dropped. She placed it in a holder mounted on the wall and took the old key in a hand that trembled. The locking mechanism was old and rusty. Eliza passed her hand over it, the rust fell away, and the key slid into the lock. Eliza turned it. I was not prepared for what was inside.

A stone platform sat in an empty room. A child slept in icy silence. A child of six or seven, tiny and perfect. "Julia," Eliza moaned. "My Julia." She turned to Jane. "This is you. This is the body you belong in."

"No," Jane cried. "I want to go home. No! I am not a child."

Jane whirled and tried to run. Eliza snatched her by the wrist and held on. "You," Eliza pointed at me. "Hold her if you ever wish to be Lilianna again. I must right this wrong. I must have my child back."

I grabbed Jane's shoulders and held her. The girl clutched me. "Abby," she said because she believed I was Abby the maid she knew. "Don't let her do this."

"You are her daughter, Jane," I said in a soothing voice. "Just as I am really Lilianna not Abby."

Jane began screaming. "No, no, I am not her daughter. I am Jane. My mother was a servant in Lord Cavendish's house. I was born twenty-five years ago. I remember every day of those years. I am not that child."

"Eliza, are you sure this is your daughter?" I asked. Fear I was aiding in a terrible travesty filled me. What was Eliza really up to?

"Of course she is Julia. I switched them when Jane was a child to save Julia's life. She's been in this room ever since. Now hold that girl."

Eliza brought out her bowl and began chanting. The child on the stone platform stirred as the bowl sang. The runes on the outside of the bowl lit and Jane's shrieks grew even louder. She twisted and turned in my grasp as she tried to escape. Suddenly, the temperature in the room plummeted. My hair lifted, fingers plucked at my clothes. Eliza's chanting stopped abruptly. "No! she screamed. No. I'm not a Bleakstone. Please don't." The bowl flew from her hands and crashed to the floor. Eliza was lifted up on ghostly hands and flung against the wall. She scrambled to her feet and reached for the bowl. "Oh, Julia, no," she cried.

The angry spirits grabbed at Eliza's clothes, tearing at them just as they had Mother's. Her hair caught on fire and Jane screamed and hid behind me. I had no idea what to do. Eliza was being murdered right before my eyes. She was naked and bleeding from many wounds. The flames from her burning hair spread to the scraps of clothing she'd worn. Jane and I leaped out of the way. I couldn't take my eyes from the bowl which now lay at the center of the conflagration. If it was destroyed. I would be Abby for the rest of my life.

In seconds, Eliza was gone. As Lichfield's body had done, it burned with blue-white heat and all that remained were ashes. The child, Julia, sat up on the stone platform. Her round eyes were filled with horror as she slowly awakened.

"The bowl, Abby," Jane said and pointed.

The runes on the side had faded. The interior of the bowl, once green gems, was now dark and covered with oily soot. I touched it. The bright exterior was cool to the touch even though it had been sitting in the center of the conflagration. I picked it up and rubbed it like Eliza had done. Nothing happened. I rubbed the soot off with my apron. A dull pewter surface was all I found. No glowing brass. No etched runes. I quickly rubbed the inside. The green-gem interior was more pewter. The magic bowl was now nothing, just an old bowl, dinged in many places, dented, the lip curled. All my hope of returning to my body and once again being Lilianna Everleigh died. Eliza was dead, the bowl, which was my only hope, destroyed.

The child sat up and slid off the stone platform. She wore old fashioned clothing, a wool dress, a cap covering her fair curls, and stout boots. She stared at the ashes of Eliza and then turned her eyes on me. I covered my mouth to hide my shriek of horror. Eliza's black eyes stared at me out of the child's immature face.

"Give me my bowl," she said in a high, childish voice.

Without thinking, I handed her the bowl. "Will it ever work again?" I asked.

She stepped daintily over the smoking ruins of her old body. "Not for quite some time, I'm afraid. Not for years, maybe centuries."

"Then I am stuck in this body forever?" My heart pounded. My head reeled with the implications. Poor Abby was forever Lilianna and I am now Abby for the rest of my life.

Eliza reborn kicked the ashes aside to reveal the Bleakstone diamonds. She picked them up and handed them to me. "If I was you, I'd take very good care of me."

Rhiannon

Ric Wasley

In ancient Wales, in the time of Celts, there was a legend of a beautiful and powerful goddess.

***

"The Celtic Moon Goddess Rhiannon was born at the first Moon Rise and is known as the Divine Queen of Faeries."

"Rhiannon is a goddess, the princess submerged in cultural darkness who lies like a shadowy creature in the realms of our dreams waiting to come to life with vigor and passion again. (Celtic Myth)

***

Denbigh - Wales - 1594

"Mother!"

The small child gave an anguished cry and rushed to the cell door, thrusting her tiny arms through the bars in a vain attempt to bury her face in her mother's tattered apron.

The bars were thick and twisted and rusted so the best she could do was pull a bit of the torn, soiled cloth through the bars and cling to it.

She noticed that the smeared and stained garment had one of her mother's remembered smells.

Her fist memories of the shoulders and breast that she had always nestled in next to the fire were the comforting smells of baking bread and the many herbs and dried flowers that her mother used in the healing potions she made.

She grew up seeing a steady stream of friends, neighbors, and sometimes even strangers from as far away as Conwy come to their cottage door desperately seeking her mother's help - for her mother was a healer. She made sick people well, and their animals too.

Her mother could cure all manner of ills.

She used willow bark to cool the fever in a whimpering child and rosemary and chamomile to ease a gripping pain in the guts of men who had gorged on too much mutton or eel pie.

But what little Mary most loved about her mother's charms and potions were the way they helped sick animals and calmed their plaintive bleats, squawks, and rumblings.

For her mother was also a Ceridwen - a white witch.

Her mother told Mary many tales of the ancient ways and how her ancestors used the magic cauldron of Inspiration and Science according to the arts of the books of the Fferyllt, to help and heal all those who came to her in need - just as her mother still did.

And all left their door happy and thankful.

Until that awful night.

The night when the dark and angry men came.

Her mother told her later that the big man, the man who had pushed her mother to the floor was the bailiff of Is Dulas. A scowling, angry man called William Griffth ap William.

He talked very loudly and rudely to her mother and then ordered her to bring them all ale. When her mother had refused he had roughly grabbed her and thrown her to the floor, yelling, "Do as your told witch or I will see you taken to Denbigh jail and put in irons this very night."

Her mother had then slowly stood up and with all of her poise and dignity gone to the pantry and returned with a large stoneware jug of ale.

Her lips had smiled when she set it on the table before them but her grey eyes were cold as December seas.

"May this brew suit your mood gentlemen."

They had laughed and ordered her to be ready to fetch another until the bailiff picked up the jug to pour and frowning cried, "Why woman there is a monstrous big fly swimming in this brew!"

The other men laughed and said it would only add to the flavor. They urged the bailiff to simply dig it out with his finger and get on with it.

But no matter how the bailiff struggled and jiggled he could not extricate the fly.

Another of the men tried to pour it out but each time the fly buzzed back into the jug until enraged, the bailiff snatched up the jug and smashed it upon the floor.

Blinking in frustration the men turned to see Mary's mother smiling at them from across the room. "What is the matter gentlemen? Is the ale not to your liking?"

"You witch!" screamed the bailiff, "You have set one of your familiars upon us in the form of a fly and I swear that I will see you taken and hanged for witchcraft before the year is out."

That hadn't happened - then. It had taken almost two years but now her mother was in jail. Condemned to hang on the morrow for witchcraft.

Her mother reached out a thin hand and stroked her hair.

Mary's eyes filled with tears when she saw that the familiar soft but strong hand of her mother had withered to a cold, thin, pale, almost frail shadow of what she remembered being pressed to her cheek and wiping away tears or fears.

Her mother must have sensed as much and withdrew her hand, hiding it beneath the folds of her dingy apron.

Her father spoke. "I've been to Marl Hall to see Mistress Conway and begged her to urge that lying villain, Sir Thomas Mostyn of Gloddaeth, to withdraw the change of witchcraft against you but all I got from her was a shake of her head before she had the servant show me the door."

Gwen regarded her husband with sadness and shook her head.

"You are a good man, John ap Morrice, and it grieves me to be a burden to you and a stain upon your name by my being named and condemned as a witch."

"You are nothing of the kind!" he cried. "You are as good a woman as ever graced the parish of Betws yn Rhos and if not for the malice and lies of Sir Thomas and his whore, Jane Conway, you would never have come to this unjust pass!"

He rubbed a rough knuckle across his right eye as he choked off the last words.

She reached through the bars and grasped his hand.

"Don't John." She said quietly.

"And don't be too hard on Jane Conway. She was never my enemy. Truth be told, when we were girls in Llandyrnog in the Vale of Clwyd we were close as sisters."

"Aye," her husband said bitterly, "and it was as a sister was it not that you went to her these two years past? When she sent from Marl Hall and begged for you to attend and comfort her? When she feared she was with child by Sir Thomas and must bear her absent husband the lord of Gloddaeth's bastard in the spring."

Gwen ferch Ellis, goodwife and renowned healer nodded. "Aye."

She smiled a small, sad smile. "And in the ways of the fey or malignant fairies as it came to pass there was in truth no pregnancy at all. It was only the vapors and guilt that had stopped her monthly courses."

The smile turned grim.

"But word had got back to Sir Thomas and he became so wrought to think that she had shared knowledge of their illicit affair with another that he sought to discredit any gossip I might let slip about the clandestine lovers."

"And so the corrupt villain accused you of witchcraft and had you brought before his friend William Hughes, the Bishop of St Asaph to be examined on the suspicion of charming." Her husband growled.

She laughed a bitter laugh.

"And of course I was guilty - was I not? For Sir Thomas produced the charm. And writ by mine own hand - clear and plain. Why I'm surprised they did not also condemn me for the sin of being a woman in the possession of the skills of reading and writing. For surely that must be as great an affront to those worthy gentlemen as the sin of trying to ease pain and suffering of man and beast through salves and herbs?"

"Aye," her husband repeated. "And the toad-bellied cowards even upheld Sir Thomas when he claimed that your simple prayer for healing was a witches' curse."

She closed her eyes and recited.

"In the name of God the Father, the Son and the holy spirit of God and the Three Marys and the three consecrated altars, And the blessed son of grace, And by the stones and by the herbs, To which the son of grace bestowed their virtue, In order that they should

defend thee, the sinner who suffered adversity, As Christ defended."

She leaned her forehead against the bars and squeezed his hand. "How can anyone see harm in that Godly a prayer?"

"No good and honest Christian ever could, my love."

Then he continued hoarsely. "But the men who set themselves up as judges and executioners are neither. They are cowards and fawning dogs who seek only to curry the favor of one highly placed."

He shook his head in sorrow more than anger.

"Thus has it ever been and thus is it likely to remain."

They were silent then - all three of them.

Finally, Gwen's gaze fell upon little Mary. So solemn and old beyond her years standing sorrowfully watching in her tiny bonnet and cloak.

She knelt down on the cold, rough granite blocks of the dank cell and pulled her only child close to her.

"Promise me, daughter. When you leave this place do not do so in sorrow - remember me in the happy times we used to have and likewise remember all that I have taught you. Do not be embittered by my fate but use the skills you have learned at my knee to aid all those good and blameless who suffer affliction through no fault of their own."

Her daughter nodded but said nothing.

"But also promise me this. When you are a woman grown do not chance your fate to others who may, through their own evils or lust for petty power, wish to use you and then sacrifice you to their twisted ambition."

The child began to cry.

"I don't understand, Mama."

Gwen stood up and spoke to little Mary as well as her husband.

"There are lands, newly discovered across the western ocean that are spoken of where it is said that good men may be able to make a home far away from the wiles of grasping nobles and fawning bishops. And I foresee a time, soon, when much as Spain does now, our own ships will sail from England to those shores in the new world to offer the promise of land and freedom to all those with the courage to seek it."

She knelt once more and enfolded her daughter in a fierce embrace.

After a moment she held the child's small face between her worn palms and whispered, "Promise me, Mary, that when that time comes, that you will be among the first that stands upon that deck and steps upon a new land where you can be forever true to all that we hold dear - beholden to no man or power save what is in your heart."

The little girl looked at her mother for a long time. The last time.

"Yes, Mama, I do so swear."

***

"Essex in the Province of the Massachusetts Bay in New England ss// Anno RR's & Reginae Gulielmi & Mariae Angliae &c Quarto Annoq'e Domini 1692"

"The Jurors for our Sover' Lord and Lady the King & Queen doe present that Sarah Cloyce Wife of Peter Cloyce of Salem -- In the County of Essex Husbandman -- In & upon the Ninth Day of the Inst September -- In the yeare aforesaid and Divers other Days and times as well before as after Certaine Detestable arts called Witch-craft and Sorceries Wickedly Mallitiously and felloniously hath used practised and Exercised At and in the Towne of Salem in the County of Essex -- aforesaid in upon and against one Rebeckah Towne of Topsfeild in the County of Essex aforesaid Single Woman -- by which said Wicked Acts the said Rebeckah Towne the Day & yeare -- aforesaid and divers other Days and times both before and after was and is Tortured Aflicted Consumed Pined Wasted and Tormented, and also for sundry other acts of Witchcraft by the said Sarah Cloyce -- Comitted and done be fore and Since that time against the Peace of our Sov'rn Lord and Lady the King & Queen theire Crowne and Dignity and the forme of the Stattute In that case made and Provided."

***

Salem Village - March 1692

"Sarah!" Her husband cut off her protests with a low but urgent growl.

"You must cease your grieving now. There is no more time left to mourn your sisters. There will be time aplenty for that once we are quit of this evil place."

Sarah Clayes dropped her damp kerchief from her face and stared back at her husband Peter. "I will never quit from grieving my dear sisters who were ripped from the bosom of our family by the evil tales of a handful of spiteful young girls, who had naught better to fritter away their idle hours than to most wantonly and wickedly damn their eternal souls by bearing false witness against a brace of most Godly and Christian women."

She drew in a deep breath and said with savage conviction, "And for that, I most solemnly curse and wish their wretched souls to eternal damnation!"

"Mama!" her daughter Sarah Elizabeth cried. "I do know those girls. Until last year two of their younger sisters were my friends."

"Friends, you say daughter?" Her mother shook her head. "How can you count those as friends whose siblings have charged your own Mam with witchcraft and had it not been for our friend, Thomas Danforth, thine own mother would have perished with your martyred aunts at the end of the hangman's rope on gallows hill."

"Sarah!" her husband hissed. "Calm yourself and mind thy tongue. And if you cannot think of the safety of your own family then at least have a care and consideration for that good man who offers us refuge on his plantation in the western wilds of his small Framingham village."

"Aye husband, and there is yet another cause for my hate. Not only have those wicked girls caused the deaths of my two beloved sisters, Rebecca and Mary, but they have forced our family to flee our homes where we have prospered since my grandmother took ship from Wales some 50 years hence."

"Yes wife, we have all suffered. Certainly your poor sisters but our family as well. For we cannot chance that those hysterical girls that flock about the daughter of the Reverend Parish will not find some pretext to resume their hysterical cries and call out again for spectral evidence of torment and persecution."

Sarah shook her head and began to turn away but he clasped her arm and held her firm.

"Mark me well wife. Should that happen, our benefactor Thomas Danforth, though he be Deputy Governor, could not again save your slender neck from the gallows, and for all that you grieve for your sisters you do not wish to follow them there. Therefore I urge you to cease your prattling and continue the packing if we are to be ready to head west when the sun rises on the morrow."

Angry defiance flashed in Sarah's eyes but then she gazed at the pale frightened face of her young daughter and bit back her retort, whispering, "Aye, we will flee but we will not forget."

***

Salem End Road - Framingham Village - April 1700

"Come here, daughter, I need your help."

The pretty but tiny 13-year-old looked up from her sewing and then rose from the broad window-seat, walked into the large kitchen, and stood before her mother.

"Here child," Sarah said. "Crush these herbs the way I showed you and then bring me the salamander that I took from the garden this morning."

Sarah Elizabeth hesitated for a moment but a stern glance from her mother sent her scurrying to the woodshed and a large clay pot where a bone-white lizard lay motionless at the bottom. She wrapped it in her handkerchief and brought it to her mother.

She didn't want to ask but couldn't help herself. "What are you doing mother? Are you going to...?"

Her mother held up a hand. "Hush!"

She swept the herbs and a strange blue powder from a vial into a small copper-bottomed pot.

"It has been 7 years since the day we were forced to flee our home in Salem Village to squire Danforth's plantation. And while we have prospered and I count us blessed in the new home that we have carved out of the wilderness here, I have not forgot my vow to repay those who murdered my sisters and falsely accused me."

She bent down and took the white salamander from her daughter.

"It is the 7th year on the 7th day since they were most cruelly and unjustly put to death by those who bore false witness and their souls do cry out to me to balance the scales and give them peace."

Sarah Elizabeth took a step back from the look of fury on her mother's face.

She turned to her. "Check the eastern sky daughter - has the moon risen?"

"It is just doing so now, mother."

"Good, then all is ready. Come."

So saying she opened the back door and stepped into the yard. It was bright with the pale white light of an enormous full moon.

There was a small fire burning in the rending pit where they boiled down hog fat to make tallow for candles and soap.

She swung the chain out from the iron tripod and attached the copper pot to it.

Then she grasped the albino salamander and with one deft motion slit its tiny throat. Sarah Elizabeth gasped but didn't speak. She only watched with wide eyes as her mother let the blood trickle into the pot while she chanted in an ancient language that Sarah Elizabeth was unfamiliar with.

Her mother sensed as much and when the chant was finished she said, "It is the language of the old

Celts, girl, from long ago when our ancestors dwelt in the dark forests and mountains of Wales - long before the coming of Christ and his teachings.

It is the tongue that calls the faerie folk and entreats their help in righting wrongs and punishing evil-doers."

"Are we punishing someone then mother?"

"No, daughter. We are fulfilling a vow and closing a circle that was breached 7 years ago when a gaggle of wicked girls did cause the death of my sisters for no better reason than to relieve their own boredom."

She watched the white, thick, fragrant smoke rise to the moon.

"And this night the consequence of those deeds will be visited upon them. And Aye... to all those who do us harm and their descendants."

***

Salem End Road - Framingham, Massachusetts - Present Day

Sarah Elizabeth Chamberlin looked at the dry rot surrounding the warped windowsill of the 300-year-old house and sighed. Fixing up this antique money pit to sell was going to take a lot more than she wanted to spend and even if she did all that she wasn't really sure what she could get for the old ancestral home.

Historical homes were always tricky. They needed just the right buyers with that rare combination of a love of charm over modern plumbing and 21st-century insulation - combined with very deep pockets.

And while this home was one of the oldest standing, continually occupied dwellings in America, to bring it up to code was going to take some very deep pockets indeed.

True, it was the only one of the original seven homes still standing on the old Danforth land-grant that had been settled by families fleeing the Salem Witch Trials over three-hundred years ago.

So that made it a genuine historical site for history buffs to swoon over - and they still did get the occasional wannabe coven of overly made-up goth girls around Halloween who came by begging to use the place for a seance or some such nonsense.

She smiled to herself. If they only knew.

Unfortunately, the allowances of even daddy-indulged teenage girls weren't going to approach what she needed to sink into this place just to break even.

She sighed again.

She was, after all, being premature. All of these considerations would have to wait until the house was no longer occupied. And the way her mother was going that could be decades!

Even though Sarah "Senior," her mother, was rapidly approaching 90 most people took her for mid-'70s or even late '60s.

She was still spry and supple in her movements with a petite toned body and despite the fact that her formerly ash-blond hair had turned silver, she still wore it with her classic peek-a-boo bang hanging over her right eye.

Sarah smiled sardonically. You had to laugh. After decades of trying every hairstyle imaginable to separate herself from her mother's look, she had for some inexplicable reason settled on almost the identical hairdo.

Well, was that really so strange?

After all, when you start out in life with the same name that had been given to each firstborn daughter for the past three hundred years was it really so farfetched that more of the ancient Towne/Clyes family matriarchal genetic traits wouldn't be passed on as well?

As far back as she had been able to trace their family line, all of the women had been petite, ash-blond, outspoken, and very, very determined.

And that had more often than not got them into more than their fair share of trouble.

In fact, several had been accused of witchcraft and some had even been hanged! Going all the way back to old Salem and strangely enough, as she had discovered while researching a term paper in college, to one of the first witches hanged in Wales!

With a heritage like that, it was a wonder that she had not only made it to the ripe old age of sixty-five but escaped the consequences of her quick and somewhat snarky tongue relatively unscathed.

Sixty-five... She certainly didn't feel it. Nary an ache nor pain. No dentures or even thinning hair. It was still thick and silky and a natural ash blond that fell, yes, over one bright green eye like a question mark.

And she also didn't look it.

And resulted in *lots* of questions. Especially from those who had known her the longest. She would sometimes catch them staring daggers of envy at her from their thickening bodies and sagging faces.

"My God - how do you stay so young?" they would ask with more jealously than real curiosity.

Even more satisfying were the looks of admiration and just the tiniest touch of lust from those of their husbands who wished that they'd hit on her back in high school when most had laughed at her and called her "shortcake" or "peanut," due to her petite underdeveloped body and child-like innocent face.

She remembered how one of the girls, the co-captain of the Cheer Squad, had made fun of her in the locker room after gym asking her what it was like to go through life with the body of a ten-year-old boy.

That was the one and only day she had run home in tears to her mother.

"Mom," she'd sobbed. "Why do I still look like a little girl? When am I going to grow up and get boobs like the other girls and have boys notice me?"

"Hush," her mother had soothed. "The women of our family have always been slow to mature and believe it or not that will turn out to be a blessing on the other end."

"I don't care about the 'other end' she had wailed. "I want to stop being miserable now!"

Her mother had thought for a moment and finally nodded. "Then maybe it's time."

She got up and led her into the kitchen to the rack of antique cookware hanging on the far wall.

"Hand me down that old copper pot."

***

That was the day Sarah learned that the simple 'white magic' she'd been taught as a child could have a more personal and self-interested side that went beyond changing the color of a mouse's fur or giving flower petals rainbow hues.

Those had been fun activities for a rainy day, like finger painting or baking brownies with mom.

But on that day back in high school, an angst-ridden sophomore had been shown her the first real glimpse of what the ancient family talent could offer someone ambitious enough to realize it.

That was the day that her mother had recited to her the ancient myth of the Phoenix and how their family roots traced all the way to the legends of the ancient Celts and in particular the Welsh witch/goddess, Rhiannon.

As she selected dusty old bundles of herbs and powders wrapped in paper twists her mother had recounted the legends she had been taught by her mother and her mother's mother and all of the other family matriarchs stretching back into the dim past.

"Grind these up." She'd told Sarah, handing her a handful of bitter dried herbs and the old stone mortar and pestle.

As her mother slowly added a dark green liquid to the copper pot and stirred she recited the passed-down stories she'd learned as a girl.

"Rhiannon is a Welsh Horse Goddess, her name means White Witch or Great Queen. She is an inspiring figure to invoke for Poets, Artists, and Singers. She possesses deep magic and can manifest her dreams and desires for the good of all. She is a good witch, a Healer. She travels on a powerful white horse with her mysterious birds that possess healing powers. These birds are magical, for they are the birds of Sweetest Song and she is their mistress. The birds of Rhíannon, can bring the dead back to life and put the living to sleep."

Soon a fragrant, slightly bitter smoke began to gather around the old dark, wooden beams of the kitchen ceiling but her mother seemed not to noticed and she continued to recite...

"The cult of Rhiannon was also linked to another bird - the Phoenix, which was said to have a lifespan of 500 to 1000 years. Only one Phoenix was alive at any one time and on the death of its parent, a splendid new bird was born through Star Fire and from Sacred Flame. The Phoenix had the sweetest song of all the birds and its tears had immense healing properties. The Phoenix manifests the eternal cycle of time and existence, symbolizing the importance of old endings and new beginnings, with the extra element of starting each rebirth at a higher level.

The Phoenix heralds that the time has come for you to be reborn in mind, body, and spirit, to slough off your old life in order to face important new challenges. You must not feel daunted for you will arise stronger and more beautiful from the ashes of your old self, empowering you to achieve new heights. The Phoenix reminds you that the essence of all things in this reality, may be transmuted but not destroyed, for life is everlasting."

She stopped and gazed intently at her daughter. "And this is the most important lesson of all... all things in this reality may be transmuted but not destroyed, for life is everlasting."

She continued to hold her eyes and repeated softly, "Transmuted but not destroyed. For that is the essence."

"Is that what we're doing mama?" she'd whispered.

"Yes." She nodded. "And that is why it's white magic. We seek no harm. Only a request for the goddesses blessing to help nature along a bit with some changes that would likely occur anyway."

She smiled and winked.

"We're just giving them a little nudge in the right direction."

She'd taken the pot off the stove and sprinkled a pinch of bright powder into it, then asked, "Is Constant Comment still your favorite tea?"

Sarah had nodded and her mother poured the mixture into a bright yellow mug, adding the tea bag and hot water.

"Follow me," her mother said.

She led her to the small east-facing parlor where the light from a just rising moon was pouring through the antique bottle-glass windowpanes.

There she pulled out a small round oak pedestal table and placed a white lace cloth over it. Next, she arranged five white candles in a circle around several small hand-carved figures of birds and horses.

Finally, she placed two chairs on either side and took both of her daughter's hands.

"Now drink and repeat after me."

Sarah did so and took a long drink from the mug. It was bitter and sweet all at the same time, while her mother chanted. "We honor Rhiannon who comforts and aids those in crisis. Her sweet song eases us and gives us the closure we need to move on in our lives."

She kept her eyes closed but whispered to her daughter, "close your eyes and repeat each line while fixing your heart on what you wish."

"Hail Rhiannon, Lady of the White Horse!

RHIANNON

Hail Rhiannon, wife of Pwyll,
Headstrong and proud, you teach us that nothing
is impossible if we believe.
Hail Rhiannon, wife of Manannan,
Older and wiser, you teach us
To seek wisdom as well as courage.
Hail Rhiannon, Lady of Inspiration,
Fiery and passionate, you teach us
That in order to gain one's dreams
One need not compromise one's soul.
Seeker of the horizon,
Show me the road.
Aid me in
My race to the goal."

When the chant ended they sat like that for some time before her mother blew out the candles, touched her face, and smiled.

"Now go to bed little one and let's see what tomorrow brings."

***

And it had.
Everything she had prayed for.
Not at first or course - or all at once.

189

In fact, when she'd jumped out of bed and run to the full-length mirror her only reaction had been an angry, "Shit!"

So much for dumb goddesses and silly-ass witches brews.

She was still the same old dopey looking skinny girl that no one would ever look twice at.

She said as much to her mother when she'd moped downstairs and pouted her way through her cornflakes.

But rather than being hurt or arguing with her, her mother only smiled and said, "Give it time dear. Good things don't happen overnight." Then she gave her an uncharacteristic wink. "But sometimes they do make a start."

She'd been too pissed and sullen to say anything back. She just grabbed her book bag and stomped off to the bus.

It wasn't until lunch when Jimmy Campbell had stepped back a pace in the lunch line and let her go first with a grinning, "ladies first," that she'd been surprised.

Then in the gym, she'd noticed that the ugly maroon sweatpants felt a little less baggy in the hips and the stuck-up cheer co-captain, Sherry Foster, had looked at her funny.

She'd then lingered for a minute and studied her reflection in the steamed-up mirror. Was her bony face just a bit fuller and were those stupid brown freckles just a bit lighter?

She thought about it all the way home on the bus but didn't say anything to her mother, who likewise made no comments except the usual boring parent BS about school and friends.

It wasn't until the next morning when she passed by the big mirror that she did a double-take.

She looked … different.

A little older but a lot less like a scrawny tomboy.

She threw off her flannel nightgown and peered at her naked reflection.

OMG - she had boobs!

Not humongous but a welcome change all the same and while her waist remained narrow her hips now had a slight flair giving her the beginning of a cute little figure.

That was confirmed in her first class, chemistry, when while asking everyone to pair up into lab partners, Mr. Tulluci, the first-year Chem teacher looked at her as if noticing her for the first time. And even better, rather than getting shunted off to her usual nerd lab partner, Ralph Potter, Marc Meadows the forward on the basketball team broke in when her name was read saying, "Hey Sarah, what say you and me put in some Bunsen burner time together."

She giggled and Sherry Foster gave her a dirty look.

From then on everything seemed to fall into place.

She became pretty and popular.

Oh, not overnight.

She didn't wake up the next day to find every boy in the school following her around like lost puppy dogs. But a couple did.

And by the end of the school year, they were starting to call the house and the ones with licenses and cars were taking her out to dances and for pizza.

By the end of her junior year, while Sherry was prom queen and she was not, she still had three cute guys to choose from - two of whom got into a fight in the cafeteria over who would take her.

When she graduated with respectable if not outstanding grades and chose a partial scholarship to a top school in Ohio, she found herself breaking up with one boy and telling the other they would write and call but it was "ok to see other people".

The night before she left for college she sat in the old parlor drinking tea with her mother.

Mom had smiled and pushed a small wooden box across the table to her.

Inside were three objects - a horse and a bird carved out of wood, worn and polished by much handling over many years. And a silver, three quarter moon pendant hung on a delicate silver chain.

She held it up.

"Mom, it's beautiful. Thank you so much."

Her mother squeezed her hand.

"It was my mother's and her mother's and mine and now it comes down to you as it has through all the women of our line back to the beginning - just as it should."

She picked up the wooden figures of the horse and the bird.

"And these ... just in case." She placed them back in the box.

Suddenly she looked serious.

"But promise me. You will be very careful and very, very sparing on how you use them."

Startled at the intensity of her mother's stare, she hadn't replied.

"Promise me!"

Taken aback she blurted out, "Of course - certainly!"

Her mother stared at her, gripped her hand, and then slowly let her breath out.

"Thank you."

She gave her daughter one last unfathomable gaze. "Because never forget all magic comes with a price."

***

And it did.

But she didn't learn that until later - much later.

And now it seems that 'bill' was about to come due. Because in addition to swallowing the bitter pill of having to admit that she needed her mother's help again, she knew that she was far in arrears when it came to the reckoning of all the 'profit' she had taken from what her mother had taught her from the first innocent days of the white magic to... well - that which was not quite so white anymore.

Truth was, though she'd given lip service to her mother's admonition, deep down in her hidden heart she truly thought that bill would never come due.

For years... no, decades, she'd lived a relatively charmed life. Maybe not a stunning beauty in the 'femme fatal' sense, but certainly adorable cuteness enough to send legions of men - young, old, sensible, and silly bending to her will, acceding to her requests, and generally falling over themselves to make her happy. Including a pair of ex-husbands and one current failing but indulgent octogenarian whose few remaining pleasures consisted of giving her whatever she wanted - be it material possessions or attractive lovers.

Therefore, she supposed she shouldn't have been concerning herself with selling off the old 'family manse' that had housed three centuries of Sarah named white witches. But she was.

And the more she wandered through the dimly lit rooms of the old place, the more she wondered if she would sell it at all.

She knew what her mother would say about selling. "No - Never!"

And of course, that was the largest part of why she had originally decided that she would.

But the more she considered, the more she realized that she was behaving like the teenage girl she'd been when she'd first learned how to bend natural forces to her own will. Only thinking of herself and her own independence.

What about the other 'Sarah's' who came after her?

Legally she was it. The end of the line.

But she had never cared for legal or for that matter, social conventions.

So when she'd had her one and only child - a daughter of course - a passionate but passing fling in her sophomore year, there and been no thought of keeping it. She wasn't about to let an inconvenient pregnancy derail all her dreams and plans. But at the same time, there was something that made her reject her roommate's advice to go to the local clinic and 'get rid of it'.

Sure there was counseling and 'homes' and adoption mills but she'd taken a third way. The road less traveled. The way known only to a few. And of course - her mother. And that might be a problem.

She certainly loved her mother - though her love had moved on from the childhood 'mommy worship' to a familial kind of respect. But over the past 40 years, she'd had to conclude that her mother belonged to those dimly remembered generations of adepts that stretched back to the aboriginal Celtic pagans that first teased out the secrets to manipulating the elements to their desired outcomes.

Of course, that was total bullshit.

It was only through lack of modern scientific principles that her ancient ancestors had not realized that it wasn't Empedocles's four elements of earth, air, fire, and water that was the goal of their manipulation, but that the actual power was manifested in the modern theory of Quantum Mechanics.

That is why she had changed her major from her romantic ideal of herself as a budding poetess in her freshman and sophomore year, to the quest for true power at the end of her junior year.

That had been her watershed moment.

There had been decisions to make.

Big decisions.

Life decisions.

Being a mommy and wife.

Or... the person who was going to drive back thousands of years of darkness and superstition and bring science to stamp out and rule the supernatural.

Science instead of ignorance - the ignorance that had sentenced the women of her family to death all too often over the last 500 years.

Science over superstition.

She had chosen science.

But of course all of the science and enlightenment that all of the universities in the world could boast meant nothing without the means to that end.

And now as it had always been, that means was wrapped around the twin pillars of money and power.

Thus upon graduation with degrees in physics and microbiology she had not made the mistake of so many other intellectually brilliant but practically naive women had made.

She did not begin her career as a lab nerd in a white coat and horned rimmed glasses. She had gone straight to the seat of power. The weak but oh so malleable son of the founder of the top biological research and pharmaceutical company on the East Coast. And as she'd learned at her mother's knee and through her own arcane research it wasn't necessarily a brilliant mind that men of power were attracted to. More often than not it was a pretty smile and a nice ass.

She had all three.

And she had used them well.

Six months after being hired she was dating Charles 'Chas' Chamberlin whose only claim to fame was that he was an S.O.B. - "Son of Boss."

He was of course also an S.O.B. in the classic sense as well.

But that was neither here nor there.

He was at first a charming idiot.

That devolved all too quickly into being merely an idiot.

Eight months into the tedious marriage she began planning the divorce. But first she cemented the support of the real power in the company - Warren H. Chamberlin III - COE, Chairman, and largest shareholder.

He likewise appreciated a pretty smile and a nice ass but was smart enough to see the shrewd mind behind it.

She had become his lover and confident and Chas had become irrelevant.

She sighed and picked at a scrap of old multilayered paint - most likely lead-based and now designated as hazardous - from the warped windowsill and sighed. Getting this old place up to a modern code to have a chance of selling was going to be depressingly time consuming and expensive.

And for the first time, she realized that she was running out of time to have, "that" particular conversation with her mother.

She brushed the old paint off her hands and started to walk back to the dark beamed kitchen. Then she stopped.

No... perhaps there was another conversation she needed to have first.

She nodded to herself.

Yes. Definitely.

The house could wait. She really didn't need the money. Old lover number Three had seen to that.

No, there was something she needed far more.

She crossed through the dining room towards the front door and glanced in the antique mirror.

It was dark and muddy and chipped with streaks and swirls of ancient imperfections - but even so...

Yes. She needed to have that conversation far sooner than later.

And now was the time for sooner.

***

"Mom?"

The inquiry seemed to be absorbed by the old wood beams and yellowed plaster walls of the house so that she wasn't surprised when there was no response.

After all, she hadn't knocked when she'd arrived a half hour ago - she'd simply let herself in with the same key she'd had since childhood. And the fact that the front door had been locked didn't mean her mother wasn'there. She knew all too well that locked doors were merely a precaution to what was inside - not outside.

"Mom!" She called again up the stairs, but there was only silence. Her mother was probably gone. Spiritually - though not necessarily physically.

She didn't want to have to repeat the forty-minute drive from the big brownstone on Beacon Street in Brookline out to the wilds of northwest

Framingham so she sighed and walked up the narrow back stairs to the second-floor bedrooms.

She paused a moment when she passed by her girlhood bedroom but she'd left that along with her girlhood almost fifty years ago so it was more irrelevant to her now than the history of Babylon had been in high school.

She quickly passed it by and proceeded to her parent's bedroom. Parents... for the most part average enough. Although her father, as with most of the males in their linage, had not defied age as well as her mother. So she'd become an only child of an only parent just about the same time she'd checked out of her teenage bedroom.

That's when she'd learned that men were fleeting. They come into your life on a rushing tide of love and lust and receded on the ebb of boredom and disillusion just as quickly.

It was also the same time she learned what controlled those tides... the moon.

And how to access the power of the moon - the cold silver light, the night, the silence, and the erotic magic that could make an adept the master of the vagaries of men.

Through the ancient Welsh Goddess and the first of her line... Rhiannon. The silver goddess of the Moon - taken by the sky.

All this she had learned first from her mother and then in her study of the arcane arts and finally through covens.

She snorted a silent laugh to herself as she recalled those pathetic, mousey little 'wanna-be' witches who watched, "Charmed" and "Practical Magic", and dreamed of being Nichole Kiddmann in a sexy Halloween costume but most often wound up looking like insecure, sad sluts.

None of them - not even the few poser covens she'd found in Salem, really had the slightest idea of what they were doing.

She sighed and blew a wayward strand of hair away from her right eye.

No...there was only one person who could show her the way back to that primal source of true power and that's why she was here.

***

"Mom?" She called again and turned the glass doorknob on the old hand-hewn dark wood door showing through 300 years of chipped and peeling paint.

Her mother was stretched out on the old four-poster bed with the yellowed antique lace ruffle around the top frame. She lay unmoving on the intricate Belgium needlepoint coverlet.

Her back was straight - hands folded and pressed tight against her chest - eyes closed - but face serene.

She paused, silently observing, and thought dispassionately that she would have been scared had she not grown up with her first conscious memories of her mother in similar trances. Much the same as other girl's mothers taking an afternoon nap.

She waited patiently, well at least patiently for her, for her mother to acknowledge her.

From childhood, she had been sternly admonished from waking her mother from her foray to the astral plane unless it was something urgent.

She sighed.

Well, this was urgent.

Perhaps not from her mother's point of view from how she'd been taught when she was a girl, but now she was no longer a girl.

And since her time was valuable and her mother was merely counting down the minutes until her old clock stopped, she figured that her needs superseded those which technically had an eternity to matriculate.

So she crossed to the bed and squeezed her mother's shoulder.

Her eyelids fluttered open.

"Sarah." She came instantly awake with no confusion or the normal disorientation that interrupted sleep usually brought.

This wasn't surprising to Sarah since she knew that she'd not been asleep at all. She had been on the astral plane. She just didn't know where, or why.

No time for that now. She needed answers.

She sat down on the bed and bent closer to her mother.

"Sorry for interrupting you mom but I just need a bit of help with a rather intricate casting that I don't seem to have quite right."

Her mother sat up, back straight, green eyes narrowed but alert.

"You're doing a casting? For whom and why?"

Sarah willed her heart to slow, keeping her expression neutral and projecting an innocent calm into her voice.

"Nothing consequential. It's just getting to be that time again when I need to give myself another 'beauty treatment'.

She said it the same way that another woman might say that she was, "going to the spa."

But of course, it wasn't a spa and it didn't involve hair, nails, or facials. Those were merely cosmetic.

This involved cosmic regeneration all the way down to the genetic level.

It was that which the white witch decedents of the goddess had available to them since legend had melded with myth and was put into words of spells and distillations of the elements stretching back to the dawn of time.

That was what her mother had taught her all those years ago when the skinny little high-school freshman she'd been had come home in tears. The tiny tom-boy girl, unremarkable and bullied until that night.

The night when her mother had shown her what it meant to be the descendant of a line of witches dating back to Salem and before that, all the way back to ancient Wales and the mythical White Witch and goddess - Rhiannon.

The spell that they had cast that night was among the most benign and whitest of magic. Designed eons ago to help young girls achieve their potential.

But as such it was limited, which she had discovered that night, was all that held all white magic from becoming the more powerful... Black.

Nothing in white magic could be achieved that was not benign for all concerned. In other words, white magic was a zero-sum game.

You could not give yourself something if it meant taking it from another.

But the cosmos, she came to realize, was in itself, a zero-sum game. And there was only so much power to go around. Which meant if you wanted more, you had to take it from someone or something else.

And right now she wanted - no, make that needed - more. And since it was all a zero-sum game that meant if she was going to win, someone else was going to have to lose.

So keeping her carefully constructed 'dutiful daughter' persona locked firmly in place she squeezed her mother's hand and said, "Mom, you must have noticed these."

She tilted her head and pointed to the crow's feet around her eyes.

"And these." She pointed to the lines at the corners of her mouth.

Her mother smiled a sad smile.

"Would you believe me if I said they give you character?"

Sarah smiled an outward smile and said lightly, "I can do without that kind of "character", mom."

Her mother shrugged and nodded.

"But what does that have to do with me? You've been doing this on your own ever since I showed you how all those years ago. What do you need me for?"

She took a deep breath.

"Truth is mom, I've come up dry from what you taught me. Using white magic I've run out of... "contributors.""

She cocked her head and concentrated on keeping a bland expression while regarding her mother. She sighed convincingly and continued. "Or at least those few who we could 'ethically' tap into from the spells you taught me."

Now her mother's indulgent smile had faded, replaced by a look of not just concern but real suspicion. "Sarah, you know damn well that we can only take a year or two from any person and it must be limited to those whose karma has placed them in debt to us."

Ah, yes. There it was. The 'gotcha' clause in the white witches' practical guide to magic. All scales must always balance.

Which meant quite simply that if someone had taken away a piece of your dignity, happiness, or self-worth you could seek redress and balance the cosmic scales by siphoning off a bit of their life force and adding to your own.

Thus that first night of the first long-ago spell her mother had cast had been directed at the same thoughtless cheerleader who had mocked and humiliated Sarah. Thus the scales of karma had been balanced by the transference of a bit of that teenage cheerleader voluptuousness and confidence to the skinny, sad young girl who had none.

That had been the first time.

But there had been others.

And though her mother hadn't known it - over the years, many others.

And with those spells came beauty, success, wealth, and power.

Never too much at one time. Never so much that anyone would notice. Never from the same person twice and most importantly never so much as to evoke the interest of the old gods ... or goddesses.

She had been careful. But now there was a problem.

She was running out of time, or to be more specific - she was running out of, 'contributors'.

When you were reasonably wealthy and pretty and powerful, those who deliberately chose to trample on your karma became fewer and farther between.

The dumb ones went first.

Then the spiteful, then the jealous until those who remained became circumspect and left you alone. Well alone

Until there were none.

And now she had run out.

But she still needed to rejuvenate. And that's why she needed her mother.

***

Her mother was still regarding her with a slight cock of her head as though appraising a painting whose authenticity she was trying to judge. So much so that Sarah wanted to blurt out that classic complaint from all daughters to mothers since the beginning of time, "Don't judge me, Mom!" But she said nothing. Instead, she waited for the conclusion of that judging by wondering just how far her mother could plumb the depths of her soul.

When she was a girl those depths had seemed to be limitless and there was nothing she could hide from that all-seeing gaze. But over half a century she had plumbed a few depths of her own and had gleaned some very efficacious techniques for masking what was really going on behind her own emerald green eyes. The question was - how deep could her mother penetrate those secrets?

Her mother's eyes remained steady on hers and for a moment she was afraid the answer was, "to the very bottom."

But then finally her mother dropped her gaze and sighed. "Just exactly what is it you need from me, Sarah?"

Sarah breathed a sigh of relief but didn't let it show. "I'm working on a spell, Mom. A new spell." She paused. "No, on second thought make that an old spell - a very old spell."

"What kind of spell and just how old?" her mother asked skeptically.

"Very old and very powerful. In fact, as near as I can tell it goes all the way back to Celtic Britain and perhaps even earlier."

Her mother looked equal parts wary and puzzled so she smiled and asked her, "Do you remember that song you always used to sing whenever we were getting ready to perform any of the old white magic?"

Now her mother smiled. "Ah - you mean my favorite Stevie Nicks song."

Sarah nodded. "Rhiannon."

Her mother nodded back. "Of course, I always felt it was most appropriate since we were going to be calling on the goddess, to sing a song to her." She began to hum and then broke into a sweet soprano which was joined a moment later by Sarah's own rich contralto.

Her mother sighed. "How you loved that song when you were little."

And that is my cue, Sarah knew with certainty. She cleared her mind of the past half-century and channeled that guileless little girl she'd been. "That's the spell I need help with Mom. The one that goes all the way back to Rhiannon. The one that taps directly into the ancient pre-Christian magic of the Celts. The elemental magic developed long before the concept of White or Black - Good or Evil. The true elemental magic of earth, air, fire and water and everything that binds it together for human mortals to use it."

Her mother's smile froze, replaced by a cold dawning. "Blood." She said in a flat voice. "You want to use the magic of the blood spells."

"No Mom - the moon!" Sarah protested. "I want the ancient communication with the essence of the goddess under the aegis of the full moon according to the old ways."

"Yes." Her mother continued in the same flat voice. "And those old ways were sanctified only by blood. The blood of the practitioner and the blood of the sacrifice - willing or unwilling."

Sarah felt herself beginning to flush and struggled to maintain her calm.

"We've done similar spells before, Mom," she began but her mother cut her off.

"Yes, but never with blood."

Sarah started to speak but her mother held up a hand.

"And don't tell me about the pinprick in the potion. That was only symbolic and only a drop. Not like the ancient spells that call for bowls or sometimes even 'red heart's blood'. I will never condone that."

"And I'm not asking you to," Sarah said soothingly. "All I really need is some advice and clarification as to some of the texts you showed me years ago."

Her mother looked puzzled.

"You remember, Mom, the ones that came from Wales to Salem?"

Her mother bit the inside of her lip and after a long moment nodded.

"All right, I know the ones you're talking about and I suppose they're all right as long as they contain none the ancient blood spells."

She got up and moved toward the library in the North wing.

Sarah followed behind her and allowed herself a wry smile. "Yes, Mom, there are none you knew but there are in the ones I finally discovered -located in Salem. And when combined with yours ..."

***

Her mother insisted that she help her and of course, that was the last thing that Sarah wanted. So she tried to demure by saying she didn't want to tire her mother out, or place a burden on her. But she had stubbornly refused to give Sarah that original 16th Century Welsh spell unless she was present. So in the end Sarah was forced to acquiesce.

"Besides," her mother said, "You're just going to siphon a few years from someone whose karma is owed to your own."

She paused. "Who is it by the way?"

"No one you know, Mom," she answered casually, drawing on all of her skill to keep the veil behind her eyes in place. "Just some little troll from a rival company who screwed me on a deal."

She couldn't afford to have the true scope of her plan for a topic of discussion. That would never do.

So she was going to have to do some fancy juggling with the coordination of people, places, and times to keep the various parts separate and only come together at the final moment.

But she was good at that - she'd had a lifetime to practice.

***

The Night of the Blood Moon

Sarah downshifted from third to second gear and turned the Mercedes left off Route 20 onto Wayside Inn Road. The sinking autumn sun filtered through the turning foliage overhanging the rural lane, transforming the light to spots of orange, yellow, and red - the color of blood.

She glanced briefly at the girl next to her as she let her mind drift back to all the events of the past fifty years that seemed now less a clever plan than an inexorable spiral to tonight's conclusion.

Ever since that first taste of power she'd felt nothing but certainly.

Up until tonight.

But as it had turned out, when this night - the night of the Blood Moon came - she was feeling increasingly uneasy about completing all of the steps outlined in the ancient parchment she had worked so long to obtain.

She had considered herself an adept in the arcane arts but she was both chagrined and perhaps a little relieved that she had not been able to perform the final rite as mandated in the ancient text.

Yet...

And even now, she was having second thoughts about the most important part of the ritual - the sacrifice. Not for the idea behind it, but for what the rite called for.

Her daughter.

Though to be completely honest with herself, she'd certainly not be up for any awards for, "Mother of the Year'. The fact was that her daughter still didn't know that the woman she thought of as her 'Godmother' (when she was little she'd called Sarah her, 'Fairy Godmother') was in reality, her biological mother.

That title had gone to Sarah's college roommate when Sarah had gotten pregnant from her long-ago and very forgettable lover.

Her sophomore roommate, second-generation Italian immigrant, Jenna Martinelli, hadn't been very happy with college and Sarah hadn't been very happy with the idea of impending and quite unwanted, motherhood.

Oddly enough this gave the roommates an unexpected but welcome solution to both their familial problems. Jenna was a lesbian whose family expected her to marry to produce children for her large Neapolitan clan. Sarah was the talented, driven daughter of a long line of talented driven daughters.

To be sure, Sarah was expected to marry and produce a daughter, though not necessarily in that order, as had generations of Welsh witches before her. Unfortunately, Sarah had bigger dreams and more ambitious plans and no desire to wind up a martyr to motherhood as had so many of the white witches in generations past. So the reluctant mother and closet lesbian had made a mutually beneficial bargain.

Jenna, a budding feminist artist who was planning to drop out to be with her lover, would take the baby to New York and raise her as her own, thus satisfying her family's need for reproduction.

Sarah agreed - with the proviso that she would be the child's Godmother and that the girl's name, because of course it must be a girl, would be, as tradition demanded, Sarah.

***

That's why earlier that night after she had picked up her "god-daughter" from school Sarah consoled herself that she had certainly lived up to her part of the bargain. She'd provided the girl and her ersatz 'mother' with every comfort that money - or rather a string of wealthy husbands - could provide. And in return, she had enjoyed the fun of a daughter without the unpleasant weight of mothering a child. A condition that had allowed her to indulge and spoil her whenever the girl came to visit her 'Aunt Sarah'.

Truth be told, although the concept of selfless love had faded over the years, she did have to admit that the precocious little girl and charming young lady she'd become had endeared her namesake to her heart. Or at least as much of heart as she had left.

And there was the rub.

For as much as she'd prided herself on her single-minded and ruthless ambition to use all of her considerable talents to achieve her goals, she'd found that when it came to this last component of the spell she'd spent so many decades on teasing out of the ancient texts, she was not sure that she could do it.

Could she really lay her only daughter down under the light of the blood moon and slit her throat and let her 'heart's blood' fill a silver bowl to boil over a fire made from 'the wood from the holly branch' rising into the night sky to the blood-red moon?

The old texts had hinted that the ancient priestesses had sacrificed their firstborn daughter. But that implied they'd had others.

And though she'd never acknowledged her as such, she was still aware that she had only one. And as hard as she'd tried to focus on the end and not the means, she was not prepared to sacrifice that.

The spell called for the "The heart's blood of the firstborn daughter by the light of the Blood Moon" But did that really mean all of the blood - or perhaps just some? That was where she hoped to compromise the spell. That was why she needed the best Adept she knew - her mother. As far as she could tell, what she was about to do had never been done before. It was the concepts and rituals of two different spells.

One ancient pagan elemental magic, and one Christian White magic. It was rather like the formation of a new recipe or chemical compound. Her training and knowledge of the component parts made her assume that she knew what was going to happen. But then again, there was no real certainty.

So when she'd swung the Mercedes into the Salem End Road driveway and coasted to a stop in front of the old house she fought to tamp down the growing feeling of unease. Instead, she fell back on the skills she honed over many decades and merely smiled at the girl in the passenger seat. "We're here buttercup. Nana is going to be so happy to see you."

On her first visit to her mother to the old house on Salem End Road with her new 'Goddaughter', she'd introduced the little girl to her mother as Nana. And over the ensuing sixteen years, the title had been happily accepted by both surrogate granddaughter and grandmother.

"I'll be happy to see her too, Aunt Sarah," she smiled.

Sarah smiled back taking in the exclusive Boston girls prep school blue tartan skirt, blue and white striped tie, and grey flannel blazer with the Latin school motto emblazoned on the pocket.

"Well, I know she's always delighted every time you come." She murmured as she slipped the car into park and turned off the engine.

She opened the car door, stood up, and stretched. Her daughter did the same - with an unconscious mimicry so close to her own mannerism that for a moment she felt as though a shadow had passed over her grave.

"Then why don't we see her more often?" Young Sarah asked as she smoothed her chestnut curls and started for the house.

Sarah muttered something about a 'busy schedule' as she rapped once on the front door and then opened it.

"Mom?" She called

"Nana?" Her daughter echoed as she closed the front door and they made their way through the dimly lit old house.

Finally, from somewhere in the old kitchen they heard a low voice. "Come on back."

The sun was almost down and the light filtered dimly through the high windows of the shadowed parlor.

Suddenly Sarah felt a damp palm clamped around her hand and realized her daughter was frightened. And although she couldn't remember that last time she'd personally felt fear, she did feel a sense of unease that the girl who shared the blood of generations with her might actually be ... scared.

She gave a quick squeeze of reassurance in return but then let go and opened the heavy swinging door.

Her mother was standing over the ancient copper kettle. She didn't look up - only smiled and quietly murmured, "You're here."

And now it would begin.

She sincerely hoped that she had gleaned enough from the arcane pagan rites to achieve her ends without having to resort to the most extreme but chillingly ominous components of that ancient ritual.

And that's where her mother came in and that was why she was here tonight.

***

Growing up she was well aware of her mother's talents and quiet competence but she had never realized until she began to delve into the ancient texts and practice herself, just how adept her mother truly was.

In fact, one ancient practitioner of indeterminate age living alone in an old stone house perched on a windswept rock-strewn promontory in the coastal town of Prides Crossing, had told her that her mother was known through the 'Unseen World' as one of the few Mages in North America with a direct bloodline all the way back to the cult of the Moon Goddess in Celtic Britain.

That was when Sarah concluded that her only chance of success in gaining the elusive power hinted at in this oldest of rituals was with the help of two other people. Her mother, of course for her skilled connection to the past. And her daughter - for the connection to the future, which of course was the whole point of the ritual.

That also was the crux of her problem. Because while both were necessary and integral parts in what she had to do, neither was aware nor could be, of exactly what that entailed. And she was apprehensive to the point of almost certainty that should they become so, both would be unlikely to participate.

She thought wryly that if her daughter knew she would probably look at her like she was nuts before bolting never to be seen again. But that would be nothing to what her mother would do. Perhaps call the 'witch police' or turn her into a toad.

She gave a chuckle that caused both women to turn and give her quizzical looks but she covered it with a smile of greeting to her mother.

"You're in good mood tonight." Her mother said, turning back to the pot and adding more herbs before stirring.

"I always enjoy communing with the goddess, mother." She gave a disarming smile and stepped forward to the scared prep table and put down her wicker basket.

She reached in and drew out a deep jade colored tin covered with gold Chinese characters. "While I was up in Salem I picked up some of that aromatic oolong tea you like so much. Shall I make us all a cup?" she asked nonchalantly but held her breath.

"Sure," her mother answered. "Why not."

As she spooned the loose tea into the pot she glanced up at her mother who came closer and began to examine the other objects she was unloading from the bag.

Stoppered bottles filled with colored powder. Pale liquids in antique apothecary bottles with eye droppers. Several bundles bound with colored yarn. One of feathers, and four of twigs from silver birch, willow, oak, and holly trees.

There were also various colored stones, a leather bag of small animal and bird bones, a dozen candles, six black, and six red, and finally a large and highly polished shallow silver bowl.

"What's that for?" Sarah's daughter asked pointing to it.

Sarah leaned back against the counter.

"It's for scrying," she said.

When the girl's only response was a crinkling of her eyebrows in a puzzled frown Sarah sighed and said, "OK, kiddo, pull up a stool. I think it's finally time."

She glanced over at her mother who was still stirring the copper pot.

"So do you want to help me out here, mom?"

Her mother continued stirring and merely shook her head with an amused smile. "Nope. This one is all yours dear. Welcome to the wonderful world of maternal responsibility. Better late than never I suppose."

Sarah Gwen paused and looked up puzzled at her 'Nana's' use of the word, "maternal."

Sarah winced at her mother's accidental indiscretion - or was it accidental?

Her daughter, Sarah Gwen - whose middle name harkened back to the first, but not the last of their line, to be executed for witchcraft, had only ever been told bits and pieces of her connection to the occult.

She had been told that she was named after her Godmother, 'Aunt Sarah', and that the Gwen had come from that line too.

As she had grown Sarah had doled out bits and pieces of family history and the more amusing and romantic parts of the 'unseen world' along with a few parlor tricks that would amuse a child.

Then when the TV show, 'Sabrina the Teenage Witch and the Twilight series of cool, sexy teen vampires had been the rage, her daughter couldn't get enough of the whole 'witchy woman' mystique. That in turn had elevated her supposed godmother to an even higher pedestal to the point where there was literally nothing that she wouldn't do for her 'Aunt Sarah' and increase her own knowledge.

Sarah sighed. She had of course had long since told her own mother most of the details about the whole complex arrangement. Not out of any need for validation or support, but because she was all too aware that her mother had known everything from the start and thus had always treated Sarah's supposed 'god-daughter, as a granddaughter in all but name.

But what about her 'god-daughter'? How much did she suspect?

When she was little Sarah Gwen had bought into the elaborate fantasy of Godmother and surrogate aunt but as she had grown Sarah noticed an increase in probing questions and appraising glances that had led her to believe that the girl either knew or highly suspected the truth.

Either way, the time had finally come to reveal it once and for all. And that was another part of the reason they were there tonight.

She turned away from her mother and daughter. She didn't know if her daughter could read her eyes but she was afraid that despite all her skill, her mother could.

But after tonight it wouldn't matter - one way or another.

***

The moon had fully risen by the time they carried the copper kettle and the other objects out to the fieldstone and granite lined crumbling fire pit next to the gnarled, ancient oaks bordering the few remaining scraps of the old forest.

Sarah stared up at the moon as her mother showed her daughter how to arrange the various objects in the proper order that would be needed for the ritual.

Those Puritan Christians that had hanged, burned, and driven her forebears out of Wales and Salem had piously predicted that the Blood Moon, as tonight's crimson phenomenon was commonly known as, came from the Book of Joel, where it is written: "the sun will turn into darkness and the moon into blood."

But she knew the true meaning of the Blood Moon came from a time long before the pallid Christian priests with their hypocritical mewling had ever set foot in ancient Briton.

It was instead the key to the opening of a portal. A portal to the goddess. The Goddess of the Moon - Rhiannon.

She had labored for years, poured over old records, diaries, and scraps of arcane knowledge in Boston, Salem - even traveling to the ancient burial sites and stone circles in Wales.

The first bits of knowledge that she had teased out of her exhaustive studies had allowed her to expand on her mother's spells of benign balancing of the scales of Karma in reparation from those who had done her harm.

At first that consisted of what her mother taught her when she'd learned how to turn the tables on her high school tormenters by transferring some of their own charm, wit, and beauty to herself.

What her mother hadn't known, though perhaps suspected, was that she hadn't stopped with that single incident. She had later refined and increased the spell's power to transfer not just beauty and charm, but youth itself.

Not a lot. At least not at first.

A year or two here - two or three there. But oh my, how they did add up. To the point where she had scraped off about 40 years of other's lives - giving her the youth and beauty of those half her age.

But of course, that was only the beginning.

The problem was that the spell would only work on those who had done her actual harm out of malice or spite. And strange as it seemed, despite no lack of rancor from those she had bested, it was getting increasingly hard to find any who she had not struck at first.

Because just getting pissed at someone stepping on your toe in the elevator or giving you a snarky comment didn't seem to make it with the goddess.

Unless there was true harm with malice aforethought the spell simply wouldn't work.

And while she was sure many fantasied about giving her a swift kick in the butt down a long flight of stairs, her beauty and power had intimidated all of them into keeping those feeling just that... feelings. And feelings didn't cut it with the goddess either...

"Sorry girl, call me back when somebody actually does something."

That was why, as reluctant as she had been to perform the ritual, she no longer felt she had any choice. She wasn't getting any younger and she had no one she could go to, to scrape off the needed years.

Except one.

***

A cloud passed in front of the moon and the carnelian red turned to the dark dusky mire of dried blood.

She drew a deep breath as her mother said in a quiet voice, "Well, I think we're as ready as we'll ever be."

Then, uncharacteristically, her mother yawned. She shook her head. "My God, what an old lady I'm becoming. Barely nine o'clock and I'm already getting tired."

Sarah glanced at her mother. Yes, she did look sleepy. She glanced at the cup on the counter. Good - then she'd finished the tea. Not enough to knock her out, just enough to make her compliant and less likely to ask too many inconvenient questions.

She shifted her gaze to her daughter. Had she finished hers? She couldn't detect any drowsiness but then again she was younger. And again, she didn't want her sleepy - just compliment.

She stepped back and breathed in the fall night air.

"Let's begin."

Sarah bent to the old stone fire pit and lit the dry mixture of oak, holly, and birch and within minutes the aromatic smoke was curling up to the reddening moon. She looked at the other objects laid out in a circle and then directed her daughter to light the candles.

It was time.

She took a small leather-bound book of notes and ancient spells in Gaelic that harkened back to an even more ancient Celtic and began to chant.

'S gu Nasaret air dhaibh bhi tilleadh,

Suil ga'n tug iad air an gualainn

Dh* ionndrainn iad bhuap am Messiah.

'S iadsan a bha duilich, deurach,

'Nuair nach b' urrainn doibh ga sheanchas,

'S tuirseach a bha iad mu dheighinn,

Na trì là bha iad ga 'shireadh ;

'N àm 'bhi dol seachad an TeampuiU"

The light from the fire began to flicker and the smoke turned from grey to white. Then images began to dance in the smoke. A cold wind blew and carried an ancient scent of burning leaves mixed with heather and frost-rimed bogs.

She stared harder and saw a figure emerging from the swirling white smoke.

The Goddess - Rhiannon.

A voice rang sweet and pure although she couldn't be sure if she heard it with her ears or only in her mind. She glanced at her mother and daughter but they gave no sign. They only stared at the white smoke as though hypnotized.

The goddess spoke. Her voice was sweet but edged with silver and iron.

"Why have you called me here? What is your wish? And by what right do you claim this boon?"

"I am the daughter of the direct line of adepts stretching back to you through the mists of time and I have summoned you to ask that you grant me the boon of life and youth in perpetuity according to the ancient ritual."

The goddess stared back with eyes like two hard emerald chips and her silver hair swirled in the billowing smoke.

"And you know and are prepared for what that entails?"

Sarah paused a moment and then swallowed, hard. "Yes."

The goddess continued to regard her with her unblinking emerald eyes. "You have the sacrifice - she is here?"

"Yes."

"She is the true daughter born to you out of your body? Your own flesh and blood?"

She dug her fingernails into her palm, gritted her teeth, and answered, "Yes."

For a moment she stole a look at her mother and daughter but the potion had done its work well. They were still mesmerized by the smoke.

The goddess spoke. "Then take the amulet and place it in your right hand.

Sarah took the small silver figurine that had taken her forty years and almost a million dollars of her ex-husbands' money to obtain and clutched her fist around it.

"Now take your daughter's right hand in your left and step into the fire."

She took up her daughter's hand. It was cool and dry. She moved toward the fire and her daughter smiled trustingly at her.

"Wait!"

She was surprised that someone had spoken - it was herself.

"Will... will she feel - any - any pain?"

"Of course." Came the reply. "She will feel the fire of the burning. Her youth and future will be consumed in the flames and turned into smoke and all of that she will be and all of her descendants will be, will go up in smoke - and that smoke will transfer to you for all eternity. The payment for a mother willing to take the future of her begotten child and all of her descendants to come... for herself."

Her child and all her heirs, in exchange for eternity.

Suddenly all the years of studying and scheming and single-minded striving to master the arcane lore that had passed down through the generations seemed to waver in front of her.

This had been her plan since the first day of her unplanned pregnancy when she had stumbled across the ancient rite and realized that this was a much better alternative than abortion.

That had been the plan. Her plan.

Right up until this moment.

She gazed at her daughter standing next to her, a serene and trusting look on her young face.

"The future of your begotten child and all of her heirs to come..."

The words of the goddess echoed in her brain. *"The future of your begotten child and all of her heirs to come..."*

Her palms became damp and clammy but her daughters were still cool and dry.

She took one more step into the first flickering, yellow tongues of flame, and though she felt nothing but a cool tickle she noticed that the rubber soles of her daughter's pink floral sneakers were starting to smoke.

Her daughter still moved with her with no pulling back but she could see that even though the drugged tea her eyes were beginning to register pain.

Pain. In her eyes. Her daughter. Her own daughter.

Then it all shattered. All at once.

All the years of selfishness and cold, cynical calculation.

The vengeance taken, some deserved, some not.

The youth taken. Sometimes a little sometimes a lot.

The husbands taken. And more often than not, taken literally for a ride and to the cleaners.

The love taken. And worst of all - not returned.

"No!"

She heard an anguished scream and realized once again that it was her.

And with that scream, she pulled her daughter back and out of the fire.

She dropped her daughter's hand and said, "We're leaving - right now."

She began to guide her back toward the old house calling over her shoulder, "Com' on Mom, we're leaving. This is over."

"No! It is not."

The voice was still soft and deep but the tone cut through her like a knife and froze her dead in her tracks.

"As an Adept, you of all people should know that once summoned by the old ritual it cannot be closed until it is complete. You owe me a sacrifice and if it is not given willingly then it will be doubled. I will take both your mother and your daughter."

She shook her head.

"No! Not that. I know now that this is wrong. Everything I've done and taken has been wrong and selfish. What started as a hurt, lonely teenage outsider trying to balance the scales against a bully has made me worse than they ever were."

"That makes no difference." The voice sounded hollow now as if coming from a tomb.

"You have performed the ritual. You have summoned me. You have promised me a sacrifice and I cannot leave here without it."

"But... You can't. You wouldn't. My mother, my daughter. They are

innocent. You..."

"I will have a sacrifice. If not willingly then I will take it. But the ritual must be completed."

The thick white smoke swirled above the fire and then began to move to the pair of bewildered and now frightened figures cowering in back of her.

"Wait!"

Sarah moved back toward the thick, writhing smoke.

"You must have a sacrifice, but better a willing sacrifice to close the ritual - correct?"

The emerald ice chip eyes stared silently back from the smoke but Sarah knew she was right.

She took in a deep breath and said calmly, "Then take me."

The glittering green eyes flared then settled back to their unblinking gaze.

Slowly the face and form of the goddess began to coalesce around them.

"You do understand what this will entail."

It was not a question but she answered anyway. "Yes."

The goddess stared back, her silver hair floating as if in a strong current of some unseen mist-shrouded lake.

"And there will be pain."

She swallowed but again nodded, "Yes. I understand that sacrifice always demands pain."

Suddenly the white smoke thinned and she could see the goddess clearly. Silver hair, white robe, gold circlet above the bright green eyes framed by impossibly pale skin.

The goddess nodded once and her expression momentarily softened to the one that Sarah had first imagined as a child when she'd found a faded pen and ink drawing of her in an old book.

The goddess spoke again. "You have offered yourself as a willing sacrifice to close the ritual and spare your mother and daughter. And while I cannot spare your life, I can spare you the agony of the flames."

She raised her right hand as if in benediction. "You will have a death that will complete a very long circle in your heritage and if you wish, close it.

"Does that mean that the magic will end with me and not be passed on to my daughter and her descendants?"

"It does."

"Then that is what I wish. Let it all end with me."

The goddess nodded and waved her hand. "Then it shall."

"May I kiss them goodbye?"

The goddess shook her head. "No - it has already begun. Say goodbye in your heart. They will know."

She took one last long gaze at her mother and daughter and then as the thick white smoke completely enveloped her, she closed her eyes.

***

She heard voices droning in the background and then felt something thick and coarse drop over her head, coming to rest around her neck.

Sarah opened her eyes and stared out at a sea of unfamiliar faces dressed in what appeared to be Elizabethan clothing.

When she tried to raise her hands she found they were tied behind her back. Suddenly she realized what the thick, coarse material around her neck was. A rope, a hangman's noose.

She was standing on a scaffold in a town square somewhere in Elizabethan England and the Magistrate was reading out her sentence.

"Gwen ferch Ellis, you have been found guilty of the heinous and wicked crime of witchcraft and therefore have been conveyed to this place of execution to be hanged by the neck until you are dead."

The black-clad bailiff beside her piously added, "And may God have mercy on your soul."

To which the gaggle of florid faced officials lifted their eyes and hypocritically murmured, "Amen."

She almost smiled. It seemed that the goddess had a sense of humor. No, make that a sense of cosmic justice and now she understood why the goddess had said that the circle would be closed.

She had been transported back to the beginning of her maternal line. The hanging that had set in motion the chain of events that led her ancestors to come to America. And somewhere in that crowd was the daughter of she whose place she was taking. The first of the adepts that had been hanged for witchcraft causing her daughter to flee to the new world and found her line.

The minister was speaking now and the hangman had stepped forward and was tightening the noose around her neck.

He stepped back and put his hand on the lever to the trap door that would send her to her death and waited for the nod from the magistrate.

"Have you any last words to say?"

She desperately scanned the faces in the crowd for a small girl that she knew would be the daughter of this first martyr of her ancestors and then... she found her.

She knew by the tears on her face and the pain in her eyes it was her. She held the child's eyes for a moment and just before eternity opened under her feet she smiled and whispered... "I love you."

There was an instant of pain and then a tiny sliver of silver light that grew and grew and... Rhiannon.

And finally at last - at long last - she knew what it was to be ... taken by the wind.

The End

Two for Death

Francesca Quarto

The women were named after another set of twin sisters in their ancient lineage. A maternal grandmother, many, many, generations removed, and her sister, therefore, an Aunt. Those sisters lived so long ago only the family vault remembered their existence, and oddly, no one else among the numerous clan members interred therein. The words chiseled into the gray stone face of the family mausoleum, were blurred by the creeping moss that climbed the iron-banded wooden door and spread softly over the surface. It read:

*"Marked for Death, 31*st *October 1845*
Twins in Life and the Unknown that follows"

Hazel was in one of a pair of worn oak rockers, her black shawl over her lap. She sat close to the roaring fire in the huge fieldstone hearth, the heat enveloping her in comforting waves. The stiff cane work seats on both chairs was unraveling with time and constant use, and trailed the thread-bare carpet like worms on the move. The sitting-room was cozy and warm, though sparsely decorated. Her sister Ruby was bent close to the dancing flames, pushing the logs about with the blackened poker. When she straightened, she rubbed the small of her back and joined Hazel in her matching chair where she commenced to rock with a fury. After a few minutes of observing this odd behavior, Hazel's croaking voice overcame the creaking of the rockers.

"What ails you sister? You're about to launch yourself skyward with all that frantic movement."

"I'll tell you what's wrong, Hazel. We've spent our whole life in this crumbling relic of a mansion. We were born here and will certainly remain here. And further, we've never *once* had a festive occasion within these mildew-covered walls. I'm surprised you don't share my view of our stone prison, quite frankly."

Hazel stopped her own smooth rocking to study her sister closely. There was only one real difference to be found in their starkly white, albino faces. That was a rather large birth mark near the center of Ruby's forehead. Hazel used to tease her when they were at odds with one another; telling her she looked like the Cyclops from their favorite story of the dashing Ulysses. In fact, it did resemble an eye, with a dark hallo outlining an uneven brownish oval. Ruby didn't take well to being taunted about this imperfection as she called it and used her wiry white hair to cover it.

"It is meant to distinguish us Hazel," she would say, "and has given me a power you'll never possess." This comment always gave Hazel a feeling of unease at the notion of not sharing something with her twin.

The silence that followed Ruby's unusual outburst was punctuated by the shifting of the firewood within the grate. Hazel studied her twin's profile, noting the hard set of her jaw as she glared at the aggressive orange and red flames devouring the logs. She was clearly unhappy and that was enough to inspire her sister to brighten her mood, which was unsettling for her as well.

"Sister. This is Hallows' Eve. I recall, it was on this very night a few years ago, that we entertained and…"

"A few years? It's been at least fifty years by my calculations," Ruby blurted out.

"Well, perhaps. You've always been stronger at numbers than I. But never mind that, dear. I do remember what a grand time we had that night! The mansion was festooned with eye catching decorations like…"

"Old bones we took from the family plot. And ghastly displays of eviscerated cats and dogs…"

"Yes, though there was a bit of a fluff-up over missing pets from around the area."

"Oh! And remember the *children* we entertained that night? So compliant with our plans for them after they ate your dainty soul cakes." Ruby licked her lips in a long, almost sensual motion, not lost upon her twin, who mirrored her right down to the twinkle in her pink-rimmed-water-colored eyes. They sat quietly for a moment, each slowly rocking while their chairs echoed the same creaking of tired wood.

They were lost in thoughts of a Halloween that frightened even the constabulary investigating the disappearance of three young children, out begging treats together. The whole of their small town was abuzz with stories and speculations. Somehow, these always seemed to begin and end at the dilapidated residence of the old crones Hazel and Ruby Nubs.

For many folks in the backwoods Kentucky town, the sisters personified the primal fear every man, woman and child experiences when confronted with the inexplicable, the other-worldly, the evil that lurks in the darkness. The albino twins fit nicely into every category of terrifying.

There was a time in the mid-1800s, when the town was no more than a haphazard collection of shacks and rough-hewn cabins, that the God-fearing local leaders tried to ban the practice of celebrating Hallows' Eve and put an end to what was known as "souling." But the tradition of children going house to house begging for sweet "soul cakes" was deeply entrenched in the lives of the largely Irish-immigrant community and not easily uprooted by moral dictate.

Small groups of youngsters, wearing costumes and masks to fool the souls of the dead, continued to roam the quiet town every October 31st. They flitted like lost creatures, from sundown, and well into the first hours of the glow from the moon as it rode the night winds. The children always ended their foraging on the broken flagstone doorstep of Nub mansion, where according to local lore, it sat like a fairytale castle since the first settlers passed through those parts.

The forest was slowly scratching away at the crumbling stone monstrosity, with its two-faced gargoyles perched precariously on the rotting roof frame, and its tightly shuttered windows, bleeding out only the thinnest stream of living light. This treat stop was the pinnacle of the evening for the begging youngsters, even though the doors to the dark and sinister house hadn't been thrown wide in living memory of most folks, and no treats were given. Over the decades there were several sightings reported by children of starkly white faces, shining like separate moons from upper floor windows, but the heavy double doors remained closed.

This provided any rascals among them with the rare opportunity to do some mischief and make good the threat of a trick if no treat was forthcoming. To that end, many an egg or tomato made its way into a pocket or old flour sack, to be used to punish the stingy hearted sisters. This went on for several generations, as children grew and had their own offspring, and the traditions continued except for that Halloween fifty years ago.

Ruby broke into her sister's close study of the flames, wrapped inside their own breezes, and dancing like demented Court Jesters.

"We'd have to hurry to prepare our treats and decorate our house appropriately. There are only a few hours until sundown. Hazel, are you listening?"

"Yes, dear. I heard you. There's really no need to fuss over time. We already have all we need to cover our place from top to bottom in ghoulish delights! We'll resurrect everything we used on our last memorable Hallows' Eve and add some newer delights for the young people. Shall we begin sister?"

They vacated their rockers in a flurry of dated black dresses that contrasted starkly with their dead-white complexions. The heavy skirts fell to just above their laced shoe tops. The bodice of each dress covered their arms to their wrists and rose-up to just under their sagging jowls. They looked like a pair of black birds except for the blanched faces and white hands jutting out like afterthoughts on two scarecrows. They both stood a mere five feet tall, each wearing a plaited braid of coarse white hair that resembled knotted kite tails over the slight curvature of their backs. Neither was overly fond of bathing or trimming finger nails, grown so long they curled like cork screws. The most arresting aspect of the twins was the way they mirrored one another so perfectly like reflections on a still pond when Ruby's Cyclops' birthmark was hidden beneath her bangs, bangs Hazel had adopted as well.

Hazel secretly detested that mark, seeing it as a constant reminder of something she knew was forever out of her reach. Something that only Ruby could do. This truth made Hazel anxious and angry as if she'd been shut out by her twin. While she made light of her sister's "special powers" as Ruby annoyingly named them, the frivolity was only a thin disguise Hazel used to hide her true feelings. And now, fifty years after Ruby proved that power on that Hallows' Eve, Hazel had spontaneously, unthinkingly, offered a second opportunity for her sibling to be different from her.

"What was I thinking," Hazel muttered to herself as she left through the kitchen door and stepped into the late afternoon chill. She needed to retrieve the family treasure that only Ruby was able to use, though Hazel had many failed attempts. The *Book of Celtic*

Mysticism was hidden in the family crypt. Written thousands of years ago, the book, actually only sheaves of yellowed parchment crammed into a leather satchel, found its way into a long line of Nubs when it was stolen by Edvart Nubs. Family history retold how he purloined it from the Druid high priest's living quarters, while the holy man was overseeing the ritual celebrating and important seasonal ritual.

Samhain, the summer's end and the coming of winter. The Celts believed the veil separating the living and the dead was easily rent during this season, and the dead could more easily walk among them. Every year, Hazel and Ruby acknowledged their Druid ancestry by performing the important tasks of stocking up for the winter months ahead, slaughtering a few of their neighbor's cows (a crime that went unsolved still) and burning the bones of the beasts after taking the best cuts for their winter stores. They were never keen on celebrating the coming of the dreary months that lay ahead, but neither wanted to be the one to break with tradition.

Standing in its own squat shadow, the mausoleum loomed above Hazel's slight form. She pulled the ragged ends of the black shawl she wore tighter around her thin shoulders. The pale braid of hair could have been an albino python wrapped around her throat as it was.

The sun was weak late in the afternoon. Any warmth it shed was lessened by a gathering of fast-moving clouds. As Hazel stepped up onto the small stoop fronting the crypt, she automatically glanced over her shoulder, where the mansion hovered like a beast feasting upon the earth's entrails. Her sister was just where she knew she'd be, staring down on her from their bedroom window.

Though the mansion boasted twenty-five rooms, the twins were never more than several feet apart. They shared a bedroom from birth, or so they were told by an old housekeeper. The woman vanished from their home around the time of another of their father's endless secret rituals. They both harbored the same unspoken fear that she may have met an untimely end in his constant search for suitable sacrificial creatures. She was still remembered fondly by the sisters.

Hazel stepped up to the warped door, carefully scrutinizing it first for any interference. The iron banding still made it appear a formidable barrier. She was relieved because they worried about local children trying to break in on a dare. She produced a heavy skeleton key and inserted it with a sure twist. The door swung open into a dank, dusty vault. A shaft of watery sunlight struggled to pierce the dense gloom but failed completely. Hazel pulled out a box of long wooden matches from a skirt pocket and set about lighting the two silver candelabras sitting on a small table by the door. They immediately cast shadows inside the square, stone room, bringing an eerie kind of sputtering life to this chamber for the dead. Even Hazel's small figure grew to monstrous proportions as she lifted one set and started toward the back wall of the vault.

The movement of her heavy skirt sweeping through the high piles of dust and rodent droppings caused a stir within the tightly sealed structure. The eddies of air currents seemed to breathe life into the residents of this charnel house, for soon, a whispering began to emerge from among the deeper shadows around her. Rather than becoming alarmed, Hazel merely harrumphed her displeasure at having to share even this stale and rotted breath with those family members interred within the walls. She knew them all. Nubs of every time and description resided within, their lives having been spent as feverishly as coin on cheap liquor, in most cases. Ruby and Hazel had no particular attachment to the family tree, and only this mausoleum provided any true connection to the fierce blood running through their freakishly white bodies.

Hazel went to a rectangular slot carved deep into the wall marked *Edvart Nub~ Patriarch.* She touched the side of the alcove feeling the cold slick of slime beneath her fingers. Suddenly, a narrow opening appeared in the wall. She lifted her candles higher to see more clearly and reaching in withdrew the decaying leather satchel holding the pages of the *Book of Celtic Mysticism*. She was turning toward the door when a new shadow fell across her path.

"Ruby! Why did you come out in the chill air, sister? I've no need of your help as my task is completed."

"I want to begin our preparations immediately, Hazel. We've only an hour before sunset by the look of the skies. Let's awaken the others and get them arranged in the house before the tykes brave their yearly visit this Hallows' Eve. Finding some children here already will surely make them less fearful."

She was laughing and seemed happier than Hazel had seen her in many a lifetime spent in the Nubs mansion. It would have warmed her heart if she had one that beat with the thrill of human existence. But that feeling of exhilaration was long snuffed out, lost in the fog of history; remarked upon only in the annals of the book she held in her gnarled fingers. She reached out to the starkly white face of her twin and gently touched her withered cheek with a cold hand. Even to Hazel's rheumy eyes, Ruby's skin glowed with a surprising unworldly luminescence.

"And so we shall, dear. Let's get indoors and out of this dust bin!"

Slamming the heavy door, they both heard the whispers rising in volume, imploring them to return.

"Ignore the others, Ruby. This night only a few should be allowed to leave the crypt. Having all of them proved much too frightening to the children when last we celebrated our sacred rites."

"I believe it was more the preparations for feasting on the plump one that turned the others a bit off, Hazel. Let's not repeat that mistake and save that until they've had their fill of your soul cakes. That always makes them so wonderfully docile."

"You really are thoughtful, sister. Always trying to dull the pain of others." Ruby failed to hear the sarcasm in that statement.

Taking the leather case and its spells and incantations to their favorite places in front of the fireplace, the twins moved their chairs close together. They began rocking with the same rhythm and began to search through the charms.

Only Ruby could actually bring the power of the incantations to bear, and she called these out in her raspy voice. When they rediscovered the spell for Hallows' Eve preparations, the sisters shared toothless grins as they listened to the ensuing racket from the cellar. Ruby spoke up before Hazel had a chance to boss her about in the important matter of decorating.

"The spirits must be retrieving the bones and strings of entrails we hung about so effectively those many years ago. We really should use the gallows setting for your soul cakes, Hazel, that way our visitors can watch as we chop a few heads to warm things up a bit," she added, warming herself to the coming of the innocents.

The sisters were careful not to add too much gore to the winding and overgrown path leading up their steep knoll. Most folks were unnerved enough when they crested the hill and found themselves under the mansion's hulking presence, overshadowing them like a gray monster. From their top windows, the twins were able to see the approach of visitors from any side of the stone structure. They used this advantage on many occasions to trap the unwary traveler. Such *guests* over their long years of residence were enjoying an extended stay in the darker rooms. But then, light was of no consequence to the dead.

"Just a few of our guests scattered along the trail to welcome the little beggars should do," Hazel suggested.

They agreed using the most recent guests would be best. They'd be less putrefied and more lifelike. Ruby had a knack for keeping them from decomposing completely, so they could be reused in various rituals. Finding live people was getting more difficult as reports of disappearances began to circulate around the area. The Druid ceremonies the twins practiced were mostly quite humane, never making the victim linger too long in the dying process. But it was of paramount importance to fulfill all the precise requirements of age, sex, size, and so forth. This usually meant one of the sisters had to leave their domicile and stealthily scour the town and outlying villages for the proper sacrificial victims. It was all clearly written out in the *Book of Celtic Mysticism* and they never questioned its mandates. It had, after all, led generations upon generations of Nubs into lives of outstanding longevity and good fortune--if one discounted the occasional hanging of a few Nubs who were too sloppy in their practices.

By the time the sun dipped behind their hill, the twins had all in readiness. The chosen animated dead were set about the grounds and instructed to give only mild frights to the children. "Absolutely no hair pulling, or pinching," Hazel admonished. "And no detaching of body parts to throw at them either," Ruby added wisely. She knew some of these guests were still slightly resentful of their situation.

There was a storm brewing off in the distance, and the twins watched almost reverentially as it moved closer to them. With the wind beginning to throw up the dry leaves that had been gathering over their flagstone entrance, Ruby turned to her sister saying, "It looks to be a howler in the making Hazel!" It was clear she was thrilled with nature's part in their reception.

Entering the tomb-like silence of the Great Room, the twins decided to set a certain wandering musician the task of playing dirges on their grand piano. Ruby was certain it would lend a discordant ambience and keep the young people distracted while the sisters looked them over. The musician thought of himself as a true songster, but his skills were just as limited as his intelligence. He met an untimely end when he caught one of the sisters slitting the throat of a newly acquired calf. The sister did the same to his throat when he tried to make her pay for his silence.

The bones and assorted animal entrails were hung and draped with care. When the children passed under them to enter the room they would drop down onto their heads like swooping bats. After, they would rise quickly into the vines crawling up the sides of the damp, flock-covered walls. The bones would proceed to rattle wildly, while the skulls of three Friars from a nearby Abby would moan loudly. It took Ruby years to stop them from slipping into Gregorian Chant during these performances.

Looking about herself, Ruby patted down her frazzled hair and declared them ready. "We'll let them into the Great Room where you've set up the gallows and guillotine, Hazel. They can eat your soul cakes until they come near to bursting, while you entertain them with a few of our past guests. I think hanging one and a few head detachments should do, to keep the children entertained while they eat. When they have fallen into a compliant state, we can cull out the ones we want for our Samhain rituals, and send the others home with no memories of ever stopping here. And all this shall be done well within the witching hour," she said firmly.

"And what of the families of those that don't return? The Hallows' Eve of fifty years ago we were fortunate enough to take children from among the visiting carnival folk. There were so many youngsters wandering the field below us back then." Hazel sounded melancholy at the memory.

"One of the Friars told me there is a new preacher in town and he'll hold a Revival on this night to pray the evil spirits keep away. Like we'll do, only in reverse!" They both chortled at that notion.

"Children will be taken by the devil's own he preaches, and so it will be!

We'll find out which children have parents at the Revival meeting. Those will become our newest *guests*."

It was past twilight. The purple and azure haze painting the hillside had begun to fade into thick shadows of gray and black. The younger ghouls were in position along the path leading up the hill to the Nub mansion. It was lit up with jack-o-lanterns leering jauntily from every window. All the gargoyles crowning the roof were awakened. They restlessly moved over the slate roof, their red eyes piercing the gathering dusk while their deep growls rode the rushing clouds.

Ruby summoned a Friar's body from the crypt earlier and his skull was now cradled in his arms like a bowl of punch. He had already sung part of a Requiem Mass accompanied by the musician. He was so successful Ruby ordered him to keep repeating it until the Celtic rituals were underway.

Hazel watched her sister in amazement while she flitted between the mausoleum and the kitchen, bringing other spirits in a parade of shapeless vapors behind her. She hadn't seen Ruby this excited since their successful Hallows' Eve fifty years ago. Ruby's braid had come undone in all her frantic movements. Her coarse white hair hung around her thin body, puffing out like a white sheet with every brisk movement. Only the glitter from her pale eyes and the Cyclops' mark hinted that she was no spirit.

"You look like one of the ghosts you have brought from the crypt, Ruby," Hazel commented as Ruby scurried around, sending the dead to their appointed places.

Ruby was too absorbed in her preparations to pick up the note of jealousy in her sister's voice. It was always just under the surface in their long and twisted life together. Hazel judged it unfair that Ruby was able to access the mysteries of the Druid *Book of Mysticism*, while she could only act as her assistant in any rituals. She once voiced her displeasure at the lopsided arrangement to Ruby.

"But sister, it was I who was born first and wear the special mark. The place of your own birth puts you second to me, in all things."

Hazel still chaffed under the words and implicit threat to her if she didn't recognize her sister's superior place in their cult. She walked off to sit in her chair in front of the fire, recently built up by one of the guests from the vault. She sighed deeply as she began to rock, slow and sure, like her tendencies in everything. She stopped when she reached the obvious answer to a jealousy that had been gnawing on the bone of her vanity since birth.

Suddenly, her ears picked up the mixed sound of laughter and screaming from somewhere along the path.

"The children are coming, and I must be prepared to do my part," she said to the flames and left the sitting room.

Ruby was already at the door calling to the hesitant young people. Five of them were huddled like geese, scuffing their feet and talking low among themselves. She knew they'd be hesitant to come to the mansion doors, though they were flung open and welcoming. Hazel came up beside her as quietly as the mist beginning to roll over the children's old shoes and lick at their bare ankles.

"Don't you think the fog is a bit much, Ruby?"

"Hush! They are nearly convinced to move closer."

Ruby reached behind her to take a large tray from the oldest guest in the crypt. He was an uncle so far removed only the hand floating behind her and a few skull fragments hadn't turned to dust in his slot.

She knew the children were here to beg the delicious soul cakes. Hazel's were quite scrumptious. Ruby held the silver plate out to the young beggars. When they shuffled forward slowly at first, she had time to study their various masks and costumes.

"You are all so delicious . . . that is . . . delightful . . . looking! We have so many little cakes that you may each take two."

Hazel knew Ruby was using a spell from the parchment pages to make the sour cakes made of bone ash and worms from grave plots taste like the finest pastries.

She had her own trick hidden behind her back. Passing through the kitchen she'd picked up the meat cleaver and squeezed it in her bony fingers.

The children were reaching for their second cake, rubbing shirt sleeves across their mouths and chins to clean off the sticky mess. Ruby smiled at their hungry little faces, careful not to break into a toothless grin. Hazel moved slightly to the side and behind her, watching the soul cakes she'd prepared disappear into their greedy maws.

And then something remarkable happened.

The children all screamed in a chorus of calamity as Ruby's head was neatly detached from her shoulders. It rolled until it stopped at an older boy's torn shoes causing him to howl like a banshee and bolt back down the path. The other four were racing after his retreating back. Only their familiarity of the path saved them from losing their way and wandering off the trail in their blind terror. When they were out of hearing range, Hazel knew they were far enough away to finish her work.

She called to the wraiths floating about the vestibule to lift her sister's body and for the Friar to tuck her head under his other arm. They followed her in this gruesome procession into the silence of the crypt.

"Place her in the slot with our father's bones but give me her head Friar. I have use of it."

When Ruby, sans her head, was shoved into the mostly empty burial slot in the wall, Hazel ordered them to return to their own musty holes. "I'll call when I need you."

Hazel locked the mausoleum securely. With her sister's head dripping a trail of blood in wet strings, she passed through the foyer at the front of the house. Exiting through the kitchen, she went directly to the patch of woods in back and found the Yew tree swaying in the higher breezes. She already had the *Book of Celtic Mysticism* tucked into her skirt and drawing this out, turned her sister's face, so her dead eyes fell directly onto a carefully selected page.

"Now, my dear sister, you shall call to all the phantoms and ghouls you sprinkled like bone dust and gather them here for our sacred rites."

The pale eyes in the head snapped open and rolled upward until they fell upon a familiar face, her own face, with the exception of the birthmark. A low moan came from the ragged throat and floated through the woods and into the night. Within a few minutes all the guests they harvested for their ceremonies were flitting about like bats in the darkness.

"And so, we shall begin, sister....our summers together have drawn to a close and our winters all stalk like silent death, awaiting us."

The town folk all agreed to forbid the young people to beg for treats at the Nob mansion...The tales of decapitation and ghosts were never investigated since the children were all too terrorized to return to the scene of the alleged crime. And after all, they were just children under the influence of the enchantments of All Souls Eve, or so the preacher told them that Sunday.

When other Hallows' Eve came around in a flurry of leaves and bright hunter's moons, Hazel sat in her rocker in front of the roaring fire. Her sister Ruby's head was on the other chair and the slow rhythm of the rockers calmed her while she studied the flames.

"The End Is Yet Another Form of Beginning"
The Book of Celtic Mysticism

Retribution

Robert James

Finn took off his glove and knocked on the screen door. He repeated the words that he'd been rehearsing in the car for the past hour, a final anxiety-induced attempt to not look like a serial killer or Jehovah's Witness.

When the door opened, he was ready.

"Hi, my name is –"

The woman in front of him gasped and dropped her coffee. The ceramic mug shattered, sending light brown liquid streaking across the wooden floor.

She stood in the doorway and stared.

"Please, I didn't mean to startle you." Finn raised his hands defensively. "I'm not here to sell you anything or try to convert you. My family used to live here. They cleared the land, started this farm, built this house."

Long moments passed, then the woman blinked and filled her lungs. She looked Finn directly in the eyes, as if searching for the answer to a riddle, and secured the lock on the screen door without looking away.

"What do you want?" she whispered.

"I wondered if you had found anything that might have belonged to my family – not that I want them back or anything – I've just been researching my family history and I'm curious."

"No."

She pushed down on the lock with her index finger, squeezing the blood from her fingernail.

"Grandma, what happened?" A small voice called from the other room, and a young girl came around the corner. She looked at the floor where the cup had shattered and then up at Finn. When her eyes met his, she gasped. "It's him!"

"Shush," the woman turned to the girl. "Back to the kitchen and finish your homework."

"But," the girl pointed at Finn.

"Now," the woman said sternly.

The girl looked at Finn one last time, her eyes a mix of fear and curiosity, then turned and disappeared.

Finn hesitated. At the tender age of sixty-seven, he found that knocking on stranger's doors sometimes had unintended results, but his age was usually a benefit. Generally, older people were given the benefit of the doubt, considered more of a gentle annoyance than a threat. Just the same, his wife had helped him prepare for the most obvious scenarios.

He knew exactly what to say if the woman had screamed, *'get the fuck off my property'* or *'you'd better be gone by the time I get back with my gun.'*

But this?

The look of calm terror on her face was completely unexpected. Finn felt a small rush of adrenaline coil around his spine. For a moment, he considered walking away, but he hadn't come all this way to give up so easily.

He pushed aside his doubts.

"Can I help you clean that up?" Finn asked. "Again, I'm really sorry to bother you, I'm researching my family history is all. It's a gift for my kids and grandkids, and I hoped – "

"No," she repeated and started to close the door.

"Wait, please!" Finn nearly shouted. "Would it be alright if I just walked around the property and took a few pictures?"

The woman stopped and there was another awkward pause as her wide, searching eyes examined his face again.

"Fine," she said at last.

The door shut, the deadbolt engaged, and Finn was left alone on the porch. He dialed his wife Rachel and walked around the corner of the house, his boots squeaking against the snow, while the phone rang.

"Hey," she said cheerfully and slightly out of breath. Finn could hear the playful screams of his grandson in the background. "How'd it go?"

"Looks like I'll be home for dinner," Finn replied, "but the owner's letting me walk the property and take some pictures."

"Oh, I'm sorry, sweetie." Rachel said and then told her grandson to go hide again. "We kinda' figured this might happen, though, didn't we? You know, given the family history and all."

"Yeah, but I barely had a chance to tell her who I was. It was like…"

"Like what?"

"Nothing." Finn glanced back over his shoulder, and the curtains in the kitchen window snapped shut. "We can talk about it when I get home."

"Alright, I love you. Call me when you're on your way."

Finn ended their call and inhaled the crisp December air. He tried to imagine what the farm would look like in the summer – vibrant, lush and green – but he couldn't get past the snow. It clung to the apple trees in parasitic clumps and blanketed the ground like a shroud. It was hard to say what crops were slumbering under the snow, but two-thirds of the 80-acre field lay barren next to the small orchard.

It was an irregular shaped plot of land because of the small stream that crossed the northeast corner of the property. The stream separated at the base of a hill, and then reunited further north, creating a small island. Finn pulled out the plat map that he had copied in the library and held it up at eye level. Everything was laid out just as it was pictured 140 years ago, including the stream and island, labeled as a 'woodlot' on the map.

He didn't know what he expected, but it was hard not to be disappointed. The woman's strange silence meant that his questions would go unanswered today, and he stood in the snow, searching for a feeling, a glimmer of inspiration, anything that would connect him to his ancestors.

Instead, he just felt bitter.

And cold.

He flipped up the furry collar of his jacket, pulled his hat tightly over his ears, and snapped a couple of uninspired photos with his phone. He was just about to turn around and walk to his car when he noticed footprints in the snow. They followed the fence-line behind the house, and then ran along the edge of the stream to the woodlot at the back of the property. It would be a great place for a panoramic photo. Finn glanced over his shoulder at the window and then back at the snowy path.

I didn't come this far, he thought.

He could almost jump across the stream, but he didn't have to. He made his way across a makeshift pile of boards and followed the prints in the snow up the path and into the trees. When he found a good spot, he panned his phone carefully from left to right and smiled. There was something so familiar about this place. It was as if he knew how the dirt would feel under his feet, how the wind would sound in the trees, and how the sharp, cold air would hit the back of his throat when he inhaled.

Finn followed the footprints further up the path until they ended at a massive maple tree. A small, empty bowl was sitting on top of a nearby stump, droplets of frozen milk and clumps of oatmeal still clinging to its side. Right at eye level, a large knot had formed on the tree, and below it something had been carved into the bark.

Finn recognized the symbol immediately.

"What in blazes," he said to the tree.

He got out his phone and took a video of the tree and the symbol, then walked quickly back down the path. He didn't know what was going on, but something in his gut was screaming at him to run away, to go home. He had just reached his car when the front door of the house opened.

"I'm ready to talk now." The woman opened the screen door and fanned the air.

Finn walked over to the front porch steps and looked up at the woman. She had rounded the corner of middle age, but Finn couldn't place exactly how old she was. Her blonde hair, streaked with grey, was pulled back into a tight ponytail.

"I'm Finn." He held out a gloved hand.

"Luna." She touched it lightly in reply. "I'm sorry for my rude welcome. Would you like to come in for a cup of coffee?"

"That would be nice, yes." Finn stepped through the door, stepping around the remains of Luna's reaction to his face. "Again, I don't want to be a bother. Are you sure you don't want me to help you clean that up?"

"It's fine," Luna replied, and beckoned him to enter the adjoining living room. "I'll take care of it later. Cream and sugar?" She asked and disappeared into the kitchen.

"Yes, please. Both." Finn slipped out of his boots, took off his hat, and ran his hands across what was left of his thin, gray hair. He sat down on a plush chair with a flowery, yellow pattern next to the front window. "Apart from apples, what do you grow here?"

"Not everyone grows soybeans and corn," she said mechanically. "There's a good market from restaurants and schools for fresh vegetables and herbs. What I don't sell outright, I use for my products."

"Products?"

"Soaps, oils, lotions." Luna put a cup of coffee in front of Finn and then sat down. "The woodlot is full of maple trees, so I also process maple syrup, make assorted candies and the like in the Spring." She paused and looked at Finn while he did the math in his head. "I work at the local box store to make ends meet. So, how much do you know about your family, Mr. McGuire?"

"I only know what I was able to find in old newspapers and a few local history books." Finn took a slow sip of coffee, letting the warm steam linger against the end of his cold nose. "Clearly you've done some research too, since you know my last name."

"H. Charles McGuire told his wife and six children that he was going for a walk," she said plainly. "His daughter watched him go up into the trees on the hill at the back of his farm, and they never saw him again." She looked at Finn. "Did I get it right?"

"Pretty much," Finn replied and winked at the girl peeking around the corner. She had the same expectant look on her face, like she was waiting for something to happen. "Who's this?"

"My granddaughter, Ava," she turned to the girl. "Have you finished your homework and chores in the kitchen like I asked? I want them done before your mother gets here."

"I have four myself," Finn said as the girl ducked back into the kitchen. "Charles' disappearance caused quite the scandal from what I gather. There were rumors of murder, love affairs – even connections to a bank heist a few towns over – but there was no body, no note, and no explanation."

"The only thing everyone could agree on," Luna finished his thought, "is that he went away and never said goodbye."

Finn took another sip of coffee and considered how to ask about the symbol carved into the trunk of the tree. The fact that he'd seen the symbol before didn't necessarily have to be creepy. Maybe it was common. Maybe he'd just forgotten where he'd seen it before.

Maybe.

"So," he said, "up at that big tree. Was that some sort of offering?"

"It was."

"Because of the symbol?"

"Symbol?"

"Yeah, the symbol that's on the tree." Finn pulled out his phone. "Here, I took a video of it." He stared silently at his phone. The video was playing, but it was a blurry mess of light. It could have been a video of anything – or nothing. "I don't understand," he said defeated, "it was there, on the tree, right underneath that big knot hole."

"Did it have flowing lines, kind of like cursive handwriting, surrounded by round shapes in random patterns?" Luna asked.

"Yes! So, you *have* seen it, then?"

"No, not on the tree," Luna took a sip of her coffee, "never on the tree."

"But…" Finn hesitated.

"I only see it in my dreams," she said with a faraway look.

Finn blinked.

"The dreams started about a year before I bought this farm," Luna continued. "They were like an old friend, or a long-lost relative, calling me home. I'd wake up feeling like I needed to come here, to take care of the land and protect the trees up there." She dipped her finger into the creamy black liquid and rubbed it absently around the rim of her cup. "I've always felt especially connected to that tree."

"I've been seeing the symbol, too," Finn said. "It shows up in random places – the clouds, as a tattoo on someone's arm, maybe a drawing on the side of a building – but never on a tree, and always like a whisper of an idea. Like it's there, but not there. Does that make sense?"

Luna nodded.

"So, do you know what the symbol means?" Finn asked.

Luna furrowed her brow and was about to speak when a young woman barged through the front door.

"Ava? Time to go!" She stomped the snow from her boots as she came in. "What happened out here, mom?" As soon as she rounded the corner, the blood drained from her face, and she had to grab the wall to steady her legs. "Jesus, fucking, Christ – it's him!"

Having rehearsed this reaction with Luna, he knew what to do.

"Hi, I'm Finn." He smiled and waved.

"Mom?" The woman looked at Luna. "What's going on?"

"This is Finn," Luna gestured calmly with her hand. "Finn, this is my daughter, Cassidy. Finn is here researching his family history. He's a McGuire."

"Yeah, that," Cassidy stammered, "sure, that makes sense, I guess. So, does he know, then?"

"Know what?" Finn looked at Cassidy and then at Luna.

"We were just getting to know each other," Luna said. "I haven't gotten to that part yet."

"Jesus, mom," Cassidy walked sideways toward the kitchen, but bumped squarely into her daughter, who had resumed her curious perch.

"It wasn't until I lived here that I started to dream about *you*," Luna said.

"Excuse me?"

Luna smiled tightly.

"Come on," Luna stood up, "I'll show you."

Ava's face lit up, and she stomped up the stairs ahead of them. She stood outside a closed door, tapping her backside against the wall impatiently, while she waited for them to catch up.

"After you," Luna opened the door and gestured with her hand.

Finn stepped through the doorway and instantly wanted to run away. Luna's entire workshop was filled floor to ceiling with his face and the symbol he saw on the tree. Mostly paintings, but some sketches as well. The likeness was uncanny.

"Your face is kind of famous around here, McGuire." Cassidy chirped from the hallway. "We all thought you were the ghost of old H. Charles, come back to set things straight, or something."

"I don't know what to say," Finn managed. "How long has this been going on, exactly?"

"Fifteen years," Luna said.

Finn shook his head in disbelief and ran his fingertips across the nearest canvas.

"Why?" He said without looking at her.

"I don't know," Luna replied. "Maybe if we go up to the tree together, we'll see something? I can try to help you connect to the spirits that live there, though I'm not sure you need me. I think you already have a connection to the tree, probably through your great-great grandfather."

"Tree spirits, and ghosts?" Finn sighed. "That's what you think is going on?"

"The spirit called to both of us," Luna replied. "You saw the symbol on the tree, before you ever came here, and I described it to you perfectly. Don't you want to know what happened to him?"

"Can I come too, grandma?"

"No," Luna said and looked at her daughter, "your mom needs to get you home. I'm sure your dad has dinner waiting for you."

Dejected, Ava stomped down the stairs, then put on her boots and coat. Finn glanced once more at the shrine to his likeness and followed behind. Cassidy continued to look at Finn in wonder as he sat back down in the living room. She was so distracted that she stepped on part of the mug by the front door.

"Dammit," she growled.

"Are you sure you don't want some help cleaning this up?"

"Just go," Luna replied.

Finn sipped what was left of his coffee while they said their goodbyes and Luna shut the door behind them. As Luna sat down, he took out his cell phone and texted his wife. *New development – I'll be here awhile after all.*

He opened the video he took of the tree again and pushed play. It was still just a shiny blur, but this time he noticed a dark shadow go from left to right across the screen. He paused the video, advanced it slowly with his finger, and swore he saw a hand and the vague outline of a misshapen face.

"I think you might be right," he said to Luna.

"What do you mean?"

"I think there's something up there," he showed Luna the screen.

Luna's eyes grew distant, and she fidgeted with her hands. The relative comfort she had displayed since he came into the house was replaced by the same look of initial fear that she had when he met her.

"We should go up there together," she said softly.

***

Looking back, Finn would recognize all the warning signs he had missed, but by the time he and Luna got to the tree, he was so entranced that he didn't notice that she had stopped to retrieve an axe from a pile of scrap timber near the path.

He turned to ask her some banal question about how to get sap from the maple trees, just in time to see the first blow coming. He shrugged enough to deflect the impact, and the carbon-steel blade glanced off his shoulder, before gouging his scalp, just above the ear.

"What the hell!" Finn doubled over and grabbed the side of his head.

He looked at his hand, red and slippery, and realized too late what was happening. The second blow hit him squarely behind the ear on the other side of his head and he fell to ground in a heap. The world started to fade, and the sound of Luna's labored breathing echoed above the ringing in his ears, like it was coming from the end of a long tunnel.

Finn had always believed that his final thoughts on earth would be of his wife, or maybe his children or grandchildren. Like most people, his greatest fear was that he would look back on his life and relive past mistakes, racked by guilt and regret; that he would waste his final moments of lucid thought cursing a former coworker, the pushy telemarketer who tried to sell him a new telecom bundle, or the abusive mother in the grocery store checkout lane that had consumed his thoughts for three straight days back in 1992; but, as Luna delivered his death blow, burying the head of the axe into Finn's skull with a crunch, he didn't have time to think about anything.

When he lost consciousness, he floated above his body, but the world didn't fade to black as he expected. For a moment, he almost thought he could reach out and stop the next strike, pry the axe from Luna's frenzied grip, brush off his hands on the back of his pants, and walk back to his car. Instead, he began to spin, slowly at first, like a children's ride at the county fair. But soon, he spun out of control, so fast and so violent that the world began to blur. He closed his eyes – a misguided instinct left over from his corporeal form – but the vertigo chased him deeper into his mind, blocking his escape.

As the fury subsided, Finn opened his eyes to find the world had completely stopped. He stood in front of the tree, looking down at his lifeless body. His face was unrecognizable, the snow around his head streaked a dark crimson. Luna was hunched over him, a look of fearful determination on her face, clutching the axe in mid-swing like a baseball bat. Finn was mesmerized by the droplets of his blood frozen in midair, but just as he reached out to touch them, the world flickered, and a form materialized in front of the tree.

It was difficult to say what it was, exactly. It looked like a person, but its features were more delicate and elongated, with charcoal skin and slate blue eyes. It wore no clothes, but Finn couldn't tell if it was male or female, as none of the atypical human gender markers were there.

"Am I dead?" Finn asked. "What is this place?"

Finn heard something in the air around him, like the wings of a thousand birds moving simultaneously. It lilted around his ears and seemed to be speaking to him, like waves of compressed thoughts dancing on the wind before piercing his skull.

Quickly, quickly, no more waiting . . .

"Waiting, what waiting?" Finn touched the side of the tree. "Are you the tree spirit? Are you the one that called me here?" He looked down at his body and pointed. "Am I dead?"

Questions, questions, no more questions . . .

The dark form pointed through the forest, and off in the distance Finn saw a magnificent castle. It looked like something out of a fairy tale, but it was all black, and its corners and towers had the same elongated sharpness as the being he was talking to. The sky where they stood was blue, but at the castle it was red, and a pale-yellow cloud spun around the center of the fortress like a cyclone.

In an instant, Finn's surroundings changed, and they were standing in the courtyard, black stone walls rising around him like mountains. Not far from where he stood, there was a large round pool with shimmering red liquid and a towering black statue. As Finn focused, he realized it didn't contain some benign gaggle of angels or chivalric knights and fair ladies. It was a heap of black skulls, piled twenty feet into the air. The yellow cloud rotated out from the center of the pool and seemed to be feeding from the red sky above them.

Finn turned to ask his companion about the skulls and saw that a small crowd of dark forms now surrounded him.

Help us, help us, you must help us.

One of the dark forms pointed at the pile of skulls.

Stop him, stop him, you must stop him.

At the far end of the courtyard, a black metal door opened and Finn found himself being pulled along by some unseen force, floating effortlessly, inches above the black stones, across the courtyard and into a large hall. The hall was as tall as the castle itself and the walls were lined with torches that burned with dark red flames.

Finn had never seen a picture of his ancestor – no sketch or photograph had survived the passage of time – but as a group of dark forms parted and he glided to a stop in front of the throne at the far end of the room, he knew that he was looking at his great-great grandfather. He had thick black hair, and the same blue eyes as the dark forms in the room. But, unlike the naked forms surrounding Finn, he was wearing a flowing black robe that shimmered with pale red electricity.

"Are you –" Finn started to ask.

Instead of answering the obvious question, the young man sitting on the throne looked at the first dark form that Finn had met at the tree.

"I told you to bring him to me hours ago," his eyes turned red.

He held up his hand and his robe began to crackle. The dark form shuddered. Finn heard a pop and a small gurgling noise came out of its mouth. It shimmered briefly, broke apart, and then a black cloud billowed across the room and into his grandfather's outstretched hand. He closed his eyes, like he was savoring a fine wine or a sip of single-malt scotch, then another black skull fell to the floor with a thud. One of the other dark forms retrieved it and carried it out the door to the courtyard.

"I don't like to be kept waiting," he exhaled and looked at Finn.

"What . . ." Finn struggled. He'd been searching for answers for so long – digging in libraries, combing through newspapers, seeking out any shred of information about H. Charles McGuire – but now that he was standing in front of him, Finn didn't know what to say.

"You're older than I expected," his grandfather said, "but you'll do. Here," he snapped his finger and held out his palm. "Hold my hand."

Finn hesitated, and the dark forms in the room leaned in closer in anticipation. When he didn't comply, his grandfather grabbed his hand instead, and Finn began to burn, every inch of his body began to itch, and every hair on his body stood straight up.

"You're the link," Finn's grandfather said. "The blood sacrifice I needed to amplify my power. As thanks, I'm letting you choose. Stay here with me or go home."

Finn tried to break free, but he couldn't pry his hand away from his grandfather's grip. He was overwhelmed, physically and mentally. He wanted to run away, but as he looked around the room the sound of the voices pulsed through the air again.

Take it, take it, you can take it . . .

Finn understood. There was a third choice that his grandfather had not shared with him. He could steal his power, reverse his actions, restore things to how they were before he walked into the trees in 1847. It was like an instinct, something natural that lay forgotten, just out of reach, but would be easy to absorb. He merely had to bring the thought forward, and it would become reality. But in that split second, Finn's mind was consumed by a single, all-encompassing thought.

His Toyota Prius.

The car was sitting in Luna's driveway, waiting for him. Finn pictured himself getting into the car, sending his wife a text message - *I'm heading home -* and then driving away.

This wasn't his war. He didn't want to fight this battle.

He just wanted to go home.

"Home it is," his grandfather said.

***

In the next instant, Finn was back at the tree on Luna's farm. His body was gone, Luna was gone, and the tree was just a hollowed out stump. The symbol was still on the trunk, just below the knothole, but it was dark red, with streaks staining the bark that ran all the way down into the soil. The other trees in the forest had also been destroyed, leaving a dank, gray wasteland. A thin yellow mist hung over the horizon as far as Finn could see.

Luna's house was still there, but the apple trees had been replaced by black metal cylinders as big as elephants. They hummed with a high-pitched whine, then pulsed, and the air around them rotated like a pale-yellow tornado, spinning into the center of their gaping maw before slamming shut and repeating the whole process.

They whined, pulsed, and gulped, like a chorus of black metal angels.

Despite being confronted with this alien landscape, Finn held out hope that his car would be there – that he would walk around the corner of Luna's house and see it waiting for him in the driveway, just like he had remembered - but it was gone. The faint outline of the driveway was still there, but there was no grass, just red dirt and the foggy yellow mist that burned the back of his throat. He was about to knock on the front door when it flung open and a young woman smiled at him with outstretched arms.

"The link," she said, "you've arrived." She opened the door and gestured for him to come inside. "I've been waiting for you."

Finn walked in without a word, still unsure of where he was, what this was all about, or why it was happening. He thought he'd lived a good life – certainly not pious – but had always tried to make important decisions in his life with a strong moral compass. Maybe he was wrong? Maybe in the end, some all-knowing power had looked at the sum total of Finn's life, and decided he wasn't worthy.

Was this Hell?

He sat down in the front room and pictured Luna sitting across from him. The furniture was now made from the same black metal as the machines outside, and the chair was more of an egg-shaped cocoon, enveloping Finn and conforming to the shape of his body. He couldn't remember what the young woman was wearing when she opened the door, but she stood in front of him now, wearing a black robe identical to the one his grandfather had worn. Her long black hair was looped and braided into a flowing pattern, lying across her shoulder. Her blue eyes, the same shade as the dark forms from the tree, sparkled with a mix of pride and excitement.

"You honor me," she knelt in front of Finn, extended her arms to the floor and bowed her head. "We've been preparing for you."

"We?"

"My mother, and her mother's before her."

"You mean Luna?" Finn's head started to spin.

"No, she died during contact," she replied, "after fulfilling her destiny by sacrificing you to the tree spirit."

"What?"

"Here," she said and attached a small device to Finn's temple.

Images immediately flooded his mind, a blur of action and emotion that left him gasping for air. It was like the entire history of the world had just passed in front of his eyes in the span of a few seconds. He watched as the red soil and yellow mist spread out from Luna's farm like a virus. He saw riots, protests, and rebellion. He felt the fear, panic, and hatred as the world burned, and every living thing on the planet disappeared, one by one. Finn had never experienced such an overwhelming sense of loneliness. He felt utterly empty and alone.

"It's," he stared at the wall, "all gone."

"Repurposed," the young woman corrected.

"What year is it?" Finn asked.

"It's been 3,413 years since you and Luna made contact possible," she said. "You're the link. I am the guardian."

"Guardian of what?" Finn raised his voice. "Everything is gone!"

"The magic," she said sweetly and looked up. "It's everywhere, just as it was when you first came here. The world was full of magic that nobody wanted. He claimed the magic in the other world, but you and Luna gifted him the magic that flourished here."

"I didn't give him anything!" Finn protested. "I just wanted to come home."

"You are home," the girl moved closer to Finn and ran her hands across his thighs, "and together, we'll repopulate the world in his image."

"Young lady," Finn brushed her hands away, "I don't know exactly what you have in mind, but I'm old enough to be your grandfather, and besides that, I'm married, I'm...." Finn trailed off.

Rachel was gone.

She'd been gone for over 3,413 meaningless years – but it made no difference. Finn still wanted no part of his great-great grandfather's ambitions. This wasn't his life.

It wasn't his destiny.

"I'm going home," he said defiantly and stood up to leave.

"You're not Finn anymore." She got to her feet and blocked his way. "You are the link, and I am the guardian."

She touched the air in front of Finn's face, and it shimmered like a mirror. He recognized the face immediately, even though it wasn't his. He looked at his hands and ran his fingers up the side of his arm. His age spots were gone, his hair was black instead of gray, and his bicep was tight and firm.

He was young again.

"In his image," she repeated.

Finn's eyes filled with the weight of his despair, and he watched as a solitary tear traced a gentle arc down his cheek, then fell to the floor.

Tell-Tale would like to thank you for your purchase. If you would like to read more by these or other fine TT authors, please visit our website:

www.tell-talepublishing.com

About the Authors

Ric Wasley

Ric has a 40 year professional career history in advertising, publishing and marketing in Boston, New York and San Francisco. He has degrees in history and psychology and has been trained in debating, public speaking and stage acting. A large part of his 40 year career was spent in numerous professional and business settings as a presenter and featured speaker at seminars and professional meetings.

Ric has been a visiting professor at Worcester Polytech Institute. He also teaches a popular course on marketing for authors at prominent venues such as the venerable "Cape Cod Writers Conference". Ric is a published author of a Mystery Series and multiple other novels. You can visit Ric at his <u>Website</u>\

www.ricwasley.com

Francesca Quarto

Francesca is part of a large Italian family where she discovered early on that a love of reading was as much a part of her DNA as her mother's skill at baking. Growing up in a house filled with laughter, screaming, banging pots, fighting and loving family bonds, shaped her life and heart.

Having moved from the east coast where she was raised between New York and New Jersey, Francesca left for the Midwest where she spent several years outside the Chicago area raising a family of three children, completing her college degrees and writing introspective poetry like other young mothers.

Francesca has worked in local television, a small city zoo, founded a non-profit tutoring agency for an inner-city neighborhood which eventually served local school districts, worked for an International Evangelical Television and Radio Station and for a non-profit organization serving challenged adults.

Francesca Quarto resides in a small town outside of Indianapolis, Indiana with her husband Patrick. She still has a great love of the written word and while she enjoys her E-Reader immensely, she still treasures the excitement of turning the next page. See what she's up to at:

<u>http://www.celticmagic.net</u>

Rob Tucker

Author and retired business and management consultant in a wide range of industries throughout the country, Rob resides with his wife in Southern California.

He is a graduate of the University of California, Santa Barbara and of the University of California, Los Angeles with Bachelor's and Masters of Fine Arts Degrees. He is a recipient of the Samuel Goldwyn and Donald Davis Literary Awards and has also worked in advertising, corporate communications, and media production.

An affinity for family and generations pervades his novels. His works are literary and genre fiction that address the nature and importance of personal integrity. Keep track of what Rob's up to on his website:

www.rmtauthor.com

Janet Post

Janet is a self-proclaimed military brat from Hawaii. She worked as a reporter for years before retiring to write books. Horses and dogs are her passion along with writing adventure for young adults. Keep up with what's going on with her at Janet Post's Author Website:

http://jpostauthor.simplesite.com

Robert James

Robert James writes American gothic dark fantasy and horror. His stories blend historical, supernatural, and paranormal elements with measured doses of cheeky humor.

Descendent of Salem, book one of his Light of the Stars Trilogy, was published in 2020 by Tell-Tale Publishing Group.

He dreams of living in a secluded castle, protected by fire-breathing dragons and vindictive fae. Alternatively, a rustic cottage deep in the forest, surrounded by swarms of hungry mosquitoes.

Peel the onion at

http://_rjfiction.com_.

Elizabeth Alsobrooks

Since retiring from her "day" jobs, Elizabeth lives with her new personal social media editor, Tashi (AKA Lhasa Apso), and husband, Kenton, (AKA Irish-Scotsman) at the foot of the beautiful Santa Catalina Mountain Range in AZ.

She's also a fan of other great sites in AZ, such as the Grand Canyon (above pic). She loves to sit on her patio sipping coffee (or wine) and reading or brainstorming plots and enjoys the grandeur of her mountain views.

These days, she divides her writing time between urban fantasy, horror, and nonfiction. Work on her Illuminati series continues, but she loves throwing out a horror short on occasion. She grew up with a love for Shakespeare, Chaucer, Poe, Dickens, the Bronte sisters and Koontz, so her taste is as eclectic as her range. That creative passion reaches to art and sculpting, as well as learning to play the piano, now that she has time to pursue more interests she always loved. Keep up with her at:

www.elizabethalsobrooks.com

Darren Simon

Darren Simon has been a writer for much of his life. His career has included working as a journalist in Los Angeles, Israel and Southern California along the Mexican and Arizona borders. He presently works in government affairs on California water issues, teaches college English for the California Community College system, and does free-lance writing for regional magazines.

His work as an author focuses on middle grade and young adult readers to inspire them to read the way he was inspired, first by comic books and then the science fiction and fantasy novels that were so important to his youth.

He resides in California's Desert Southwest with his wife and sons.

For more information, and to contact Darren, visit his website at:

www.darren-simon.com

END